Beguiling
Miss Bennet

Titles in this series also available from Honno

Dancing with Mr Darcy
Wooing Mr Wickham

Beguiling
Miss Bennet

Stories inspired by the work of Jane Austen
selected by Lindsay Ashford and Caroline Oakley,
with a Foreword by Gillian Dow
of Chawton House Library

HONNO MODERN FICTION

First published by Honno

'Ailsa Craig', Heol y Cawl, Dinas Powys, Wales, CF64 4AH

1 2 3 4 5 6 7 8 9 10

ISBN 978-1-909983-30-4 paperback ;
978-1-909983-31-1 ebook

Published with the financial assistance of the Welsh Books Council.

Cover design: Sue Race
Printed by
Gomer Press, Llandysul, Ceredigion
www.gomer.co.uk

CONTENTS

FOREWORD

Two hundred years ago, on 8 September 1815, whilst dealing with the publication of her fourth novel *Emma*, Jane Austen wrote to her beloved sister Cassandra. The letter is addressed from their home in Chawton, a home provided to the Austen women by their brother Edward Austen, later Knight. This third brother had the good fortune to be made the heir of Thomas and Catherine Knight, distant and childless relations. Jane gives an account of a letter just received from their youngest brother Charles, who is planning a visit to the village. Her message gives a sense of the complicated logistics involved in housing their extended family in the cottage Jane and Cassandra share with their mother: 'He does not include a maid in the list to be accommodated, but if they bring one, as I suppose they will, we shall have no bed in the house even then for Charles himself – let alone Henry.' Thank goodness, then, for the 'Great House' along the road – a house that also belongs to brother Edward: 'We shall have the Gt. House quite at our command; it is to be cleared of the Papillons' servants in a day or two'.

This 'Great House', first constructed in the late sixteenth century, and now a rich blend of architectural styles and features, was once nearly lost forever. In the twentieth century, in common with other estates, inheritance taxes and increased running costs prompted a long period of decline, involving the sale of most of the outlying manor and the sub-dividing of the house into flats. In 1993, the dilapidated building was sold on a long lease to the American entrepreneur and philanthropist, Dr Sandy Lerner OBE. Ten years later, after extensive conservation work, the house was transformed and given a new lease of life for the new millennium.

Today, the 'Great House' is Chawton House Library, an internationally respected research and learning centre for the study of early women's writing from 1600 to 1830. As a registered charity with no government support, the Library is responsible for the conservation and development of its unique collection, for ensuring open access to it for the benefit of scholarship and wider society, and for raising the funds to secure its long-term sustainability. There are award-winning activities for schools, a programme of lectures, talks and conferences, and a prestigious visiting fellowship scheme which facilitates more specialised research. Chawton House Library is immensely proud to be working with Honno to publish this third collection of award-winning short stories inspired by Austen's work as a result of the short story competition held in 2014.

It seems fitting that Jane Austen is inspiring new writers – and especially new woman writers – in the twenty-first century. For although she is the most famous woman novelist of her time, she was, in fact, only one of a thriving community of early literary women who influenced and inspired each other. In fact, Austen so admired one of the other women writers in the Library collection, Frances Burney, that her name is listed as a subscriber to Burney's third novel, *Camilla* (publishing by subscription was a popular method of publication in this period). These women published not only novels, poetry and drama but also everything from travel journals to political debate. Many of the writers in our collection were famous in their day but, unlike their male counterparts, they have since been forgotten in mainstream publishing and popular culture. Chawton aims to foster understanding and research of these early women writers, restoring them to their rightful place in the history of English literature and enabling them to speak directly to – and inspire – future generations.

Chawton House Library holds over 10,000 works by and about women including rare first editions and original manuscripts. This collection gives a remarkable sense of the diversity and richness of women's writing during this time. It includes works by Mary Wollstonecraft (1759-1797), the famous philosopher who made a powerful case for women's rights, and Lady Mary Wortley Montagu (1689-1762), whose Turkish Embassy Letters, written while she was in residence in the east, circulated widely in manuscript before publication after her death. Here, a reader can discover the poetry of Ann Yearsley (1753-1806), whose poems cover such subjects as the inhumanity of the slave trade, and read it alongside the works of Margaret Cavendish (1623-1673), the Duchess of Newcastle-upon-Tyne, who published extensively on philosophy and early modern science, and wrote one of the earliest examples of science fiction.

I hope that those of you who enjoy and are inspired by this collection of short stories will visit Chawton House Library for further inspiration. The library collection is open, by appointment, to anyone who would like to use it. And the house and grounds are regularly open to visitors too. Please visit the website http://www.chawtonhouselibrary.org for further information.

Gillian Dow
Executive Director, September 2015

INTRODUCTION

The idea of a competition for stories inspired by Jane Austen and her work originated with Lindsay Ashford, an ex-Honno staffer working at Chawton House Library. It proved to be a fruitful one. This third collection of shortlisted stories includes writers from all sides of the world, male and female, writing tales set in Georgian times, in the 21st century and points between. This particular volume includes a prize winner taking advantage of the myriad forms of communication available to modern lovers and which Austen's original readers would have wondered at in 'The Wedding Planner'. Even the steampunk hero of 'The Nemesis of Meryton' might have struggled to explain the nature of the Twitter feed to Mary Bennet...though I believe Jane Austen would have enjoyed trying her hand at the pithy 140 word Tweet!

I don't profess to be an Austenite or literary expert, though I did study some of the books for a novel course I took at university many moons ago. I read my first during one summer holiday from junior school; in hindsight rather too early to catch the nuances which shine so brilliantly. However, in some ways this makes me an ideal judge for a series of short fictions taking less well-known characters as their heroines and heroes. If the story works for me – who may not be well acquainted with the original the viewpoint character is based upon – then it will work whoever reads it. But the stories have also been through the Chawton House Library filter and Lindsay's expert eye, so you can rest assured that they intend no disrespect to the author, rather the opposite. What I enjoyed most about sifting through the collection is that imaginations have been let loose to riff upon themes and personalities... What would Jane do? has become what would Frederika do, or Lydia or George? In the case of the latter that is 'no good at all': 'Gorgeous George' Wickham, as Deirdre Maher envisions him, is a predatory male with his eye not only upon the young ladies but also the main chance.

There's something for everyone in this volume from a crochety old Scotswoman who's been stymied by true love, to genuine compassion and concern from Frederick Wentworth for his new bride, Anne, and the desperate ghost of Mary Price who wishes to stay in this world and see more of it than her cloistered home allows, even if at one remove. I hope you enjoy reading it as much as I enjoyed editing it and more.

Caroline Oakley
September 2015

THE WEDDING PLANNER

Pamela Holmes

Facebook status update: Frederica Vernon is now engaged to be married to Reginald De Courcy.

Instagram: The happy couple

Text: Amelia Johnson to Frederica Vernon
'Omigod, Freds, you and Reggie? I saw the selfie. You look so happy!'

Text: Frederica to Amelia
'I'm over the moon, Ames, I can hardly believe it. Going into a meeting, email you later.'

FredV@gmail.com
To: Amelia
Subject: Reginald De Courcy
Yea, it's true, I'm going to marry him! He asked me on bended knee, natch. It was so romantic. The ring is beautiful. It belonged to his grandmother and glistens like the tears I shed!!! LOL Frederica De Courcy (to be)

Instagram: The ring

Tweet: @AmJohn
Put on your shades, girl, the ring sparkles!

Text: Frederica to Amelia
A, How can a girl be so happy one day and devastated the next? Mother's refusing to come to our wedding. How can she miss the biggest day of her only daughter's life? F

Text: Amelia to Frederica
Oh F, What's up with Susan? Thought she'd be pleased you're getting hitched. Reg is a lovely guy. A

Text: Frederica to Amelia

M's been trying to marry me off for years, anything to get me off her hands. Now I'm doing what she wants, she's refusing to stand by me. In bits. F

AmeliaJohnson@mail.com
To: Frederica
Subject: Odd

Darling, thought about you all last night. Not like Susan to miss a chance to be the centre of attention. Mother of the bride, that's a big number. Why is she behaving this way? Ames

FredV@gmail.com
To: Amelia
Subject: Re: Odd

I knew she was furious with me, I just didn't think she'd show it this way.

AmeliaJohnson@mail.com
To: Frederica
Subject: Re: Odd

How could she be cross with the sweetest daughter a mother could ever wish for?

FredV@gmail.com
To: Amelia
Subject: Secret

If I tell you, you must promise never, *ever*, to tell anyone else. I'd feel terrible. Sometimes I do things that Mother herself would be proud of. Call you at lunch.

Facebook status update: The wedding of Frederica Vernon and Reginald De Courcy will take place in June

Mobile call: Frederica Vernon to Amelia Johnson
'Hi Amelia, it's Frederica.'

'Freds, darling, you poor love. What are you going to tell me? You know you can trust me, one hundred and one per cent. Our mums are best friends and so are we. I'm going to be your chief bridesmaid, aren't I?'

'Prepare yourself, girl. Mother was having an affair with Reginald when I first met him. I'm not sure how far it had gone but she had her eye on him. And *I stopped it*.'

'How the hell did you do *that*? It's impossible to stop Susan getting what she wants, surely?'

'What? You're breaking up. My battery's flat. I'll email.'

FredV@gmail.com
To: Amelia
Subject: Cougar
It's true, I stood in her way when she wanted Reggie.

AmeliaJohnson@mail.com
To: Frederica
Subject: Re: Cougar
OMG!!! Respect, as they say. Your mother and Reg? But she's much older than him. She's got lovely eyes and looks loads younger than she is, but a mother and daughter after the same man? Must be a novel in it. Call you later.

Mobile call: Amelia to Frederica
'Hi Freds. Why haven't you told me all this before? I'm agog! Spill the beans.'

'About two years ago, do you remember that I was as an intern for my lovely Uncle Charles? He has that country stoves and Aga business… One evening they held a drinks thing for local people to come and see the showroom. Auntie Caroline's brother, Reginald, came too. The same night, Mother tips up dramatically saying she'd "escaped" from a ghastly situation. She'd been holidaying in Spain with friends, the Mainwarings, and there'd been "a bit of trouble". She had this man in tow – James Martin – who she wanted me to meet. She'd shown him photos of me, thought we'd hit it off…'

'James Martin? Isn't that the guy your mother married only last year! I'm confused..?'

'This was all the year *before* Mother and James got married. Remember how she has always been desperate to marry me off to someone with cash? With James she smelled lots of it. He's done well in property deals or something – always meant to check out what. Anyway, after that, she starts inviting him over to ours, dropping hints, you know how she is. He's OK but talks incessantly and I just didn't fancy him. I told her so and she was furious; called me the "torment of her life". The pressure was intense!'

'I do remember that time. My mum talking on the phone to Susan for hours about how difficult you were being and—'

'Meanwhile, Mother was making a beeline for Reginald. His family may have lost all their money paying inheritance tax, but she knew he still had some holiday cottages and a successful business. And he's dead handsome. So, one Sunday we were all having lunch at Charles and Caroline's. Mother was behaving badly as usual: flirting with Reggie, giggling at his jokes, that sort of thing. You know how men fall for her. Perhaps you don't but, believe me, they do.

'Anyway, when Auntie Caroline dropped a few acid remarks over the washing up I knew I was right. We had a heart to heart and she told me what had happened in Spain. She'd had a teary call from Mrs Mainwaring, saying how Mother had lain by the pool in her bikini, making eyes at Mr M who started following Mother around like a puppy, offering to rub sun lotion on her back. Mrs M was furious and insisted Mother leave.

'Must go, boss alert!'

Tweet: @FredericaV
Getting hitched Parklands Country House Hotel. Read *Pride and Prejudice* as Pemberley-style wedding and need yr ideas! #Pemberley @FredericaV

12

Tweet: @AmJohn
Top hat for Darcy, demure gown for Liz, carriage and candles @FredericaV #Pemberley @AmJohn

AmeliaJohnson@mail.com
To: Frederica
Subject: Miss B
Saw tweet. Wicked!!! Remember Lizzie B had a tricky mother so chin up. What next?

Mobile call: Frederica to Amelia
'Is this a good time, Ames…?

'So a few days later, Reg drops by our house to see Mother. Lucky for me she was still out having her hair or nails done, can't remember which. Must remember to book myself a manicure before wedding… Anyway, I told him that Mother had been flirting with someone else's husband and almost caused a divorce. At first he was furious with me, asked me what I thought I was doing, speaking so badly about my mother to someone – him – who I'd only recently met? What a big girl's blouse. Didn't frighten me at all; I think that's when I started fancying him. I told him to check it out with Caroline. So he calls his sister and she confirms everything. Said Mother had caused terrible ructions in the Mainwaring household, that they might get divorced.'

'That was brave, girl!'

'There's more! When Mother came home, Reg confronted her. It was fireworks! She showed her true colours. Said he had no business to criticise her, who did he think he was? Mocked him about his fancy family name and losing all their money. That riled him. Then she starts screaming at me, calling me an interfering cow. Reggie's face was thunderous. He left without saying anything and sent her this letter saying he didn't want to see her again.'

'Wow, Freds, it must have been weird seeing Susan get her comeuppance. How did she cope?'

'She was quiet for a few weeks. But if she was unhappy, she didn't show it. Brave really, or bonkers. Then starts dropping hints about

13

James Martin, invites him to over to ours again. I ended up going back to uni early, said I had to prepare for finals. Gotta go, Ames, speak tomorrow. Did I tell you Reggie's family used to live in Parklands, the place we're getting married? So cool! Let's talk bridesmaid's dresses.'

Tweet: @FredericaV
Desperate need for yr ideas re bridesmaid and flower girl dresses mid-June nuptials #Pemberley @FredericaV

AmeliaJohnson@mail.com
To: Frederica
Subject: You and Reg
Hi F, Remind me. How *did* you get together with Reggie in the end?
A

FredV@gmail.com
To: Amelia
Subject: Re: You and Reg
Thanks to lovely Auntie Caroline. I stayed there for Christmas last year when Mother was skiing with James. Caroline asked Reggie to stay, too. At first he was dead unfriendly but when we played 'sardines' after a boozy lunch and ended up squashed up in the broom cupboard, things got friendlier. Thinking blue for the bridesmaid's dresses, WDYT?

AmeliaJohnson@mail.com
To: Frederica
Subject: Your triumph
You've never told me all that before – Frederica taking a stand against Susan Vernon at last! We must celebrate. Blue is cool, white for you, obv? A

FredV@gmail.com
To: Amelia
Subject: Re: Your triumph

Everyone thinks I'm the shy weed who's pushed around by her mother. I did run away from school once; why does everyone always forget that? Had to stop her manipulating me and running my life. So, I scuppered her thing with Reg. Not too *mean*, just honest. But it makes me sound scheming, just like Mother, and that feels awful. Might need tricks to get her to the wedding, though. Any ideas?

AmeliaJohnson@mail.com
To: Frederica
Subject: Idea
Say Mr M will be there?

FredV@gmail.com
To: Amelia
Subject: Re: Idea
Ha-ha. Saturday to shop for dresses. Seymour Street at noon?

Instagram: Selfie of Frederica and Amelia in petticoats and chemises with thumbs up

FredV@gmail.com
To: Amelia
Subject: Fantastic day!!!
That pop-up shop is *soooo* cool, the woman got the Pemberley-thing right away. The white lawn dress will be perfect and love the bonnet with the Mechlin veil. And my Darcy in a white shirt and cravat, buff breeches and black pumps is brilliant. Wonder if he'll agree? Second fittings booked. Love, excited Lizzie B

Tweet: @FredericaV
Did Lizzie Bennet have a hen party? #Pemberley #Wedding @FredericaV

AmeliaJohnson@mail.com
To: Frederica

Subject: What's up?

Hi. You've gone quiet. No calls or emails today. Are you OK?

Text: Amelia to Frederica

Hi Fred, you didn't update your Facebook yesterday. Everything all right?

AmeliaJohnson@mail.com

To: Frederica

Subject: Reply!!!

Frederica, your mobile is switched off. People will think you are dead.

FredV@gmail.com

To: Amelia

Subject: Re: Reply!!!

Hi A, I've been sorting out important wedding things like who will sit next to Mother on the top table. Would you mind?

Mobile call: Amelia to Frederica

'This has to be quick, I'm at work, hiding in the loos. Your mother is coming to the wedding? How did you manage *that*? No probs sitting next to her, by the way.'

'Oh Ames, that's marvellous. Yea, I've been very busy. I was looking for wedding ideas, you see, and I found some *awesome* information about James Martin. Seems he used to run an events business in Suffolk; catering, marquees, fancy cars, that sort of thing. That he bankrolled some dodgy exports, avoided taxes, misused investor funds. I found him on the Companies House website. You'll never guess what. He was declared bankrupt about eight years ago…'

'What? That's terrible…'

'And he was jailed for fraud for two years! So I contacted him and suggested we needed to talk – without Mother. He took me to this lovely place for lunch, better than my usual Pret wrap. Told him what I'd found. Pathetic, really, to watch a man choke on his oyster but the maître d' whipped out a napkin so it was all sorted.

'Assured him that I would, of course, never *tell* Mother about these past misdemeanours. But I mentioned the social media we all use these days. Like Snapchat. How I could, for example, send a scan of the newspaper report on his court hearing to all my friends knowing that it would self-destruct a few minutes after they opened it. And my lovely new iPhone app: Secret. Means I can send out information *anonymously*. What fun.

'It's amazing how pale James was as we talked. Then he asked me what it was that I wanted. "Only Mother to be at our wedding," I said. "Oh, and a helicopter."'

'A helicopter?'

'I know it's not very Pemberley, but I've always harboured a fantasy of arriving at my wedding in a helicopter. It will make great photos, don't you think? My satined-foot descending from the belly of the great bird, my veil billowing in the breeze of the blades. James was sweet and agreed it would be splendid, and we had a glass of champers to celebrate. Next day my phone goes and it's Mother saying sweetly she'd *love* to come to the wedding.'

'I wonder what he said to her.'

'I don't want to know the details, Ames. I'm just happy to know that she will be there. See you at the fitting next week, darling. It's going to be a glorious wedding.'

LADIES OF ENGLAND

Marybeth Ihle

*'I am proud to say that I have a very good eye at an Adultress, for tho'
repeatedly assured that another in the same party was the She, I fixed upon
the right one from the first.' – Jane Austen*

In the winter of 1815, Mr Shepherd, a lawyer residing in Somerset,
unexpectedly found himself faced with the prospect of raising two
young grandchildren who, through a series of unfortunate
circumstances, had been left orphaned in the eyes of the world. The
boy was sent to sea, fulfilling a youthful ambition for adventure, and
the girl's education was undertaken at a modest boarding school
where she was instructed in penmanship, ornamental needlework,
music, dancing, the use of globes, and other refinements to prepare
her for her future.

That future had, of course, meant marriage, but the girl, Margaret,
by now had reached her twenty-second year without anything
approaching an offer. Therefore, when Margaret received an invitation
to spend a visit with a former schoolfellow residing in London, Mr
Shepherd considered the choices carefully. He was more than a little
reluctant to allow his granddaughter to be amongst such temptations
as London had to offer, and memories of the past plagued him for
some time. Eventually he was persuaded that any opportunity to
broaden Margaret's acquaintance should not be dismissed so he
deposited his granddaughter in Portman Square in the care of Mrs
Fowler, formerly Miss Hadley.

Margaret had her own particular reasons to accept Mrs Fowler's
invitation, the chance to see the metropolis and purchase a new gown
notwithstanding. The two had kept up a steady correspondence over
the years, and Mrs Fowler's were so often filled with the phrase 'my
brother Thomas' that a general portrait of a quiet, unassuming young
man with a promising career in the law was painted for Margaret. She
was not romantic by habit, but she saw in Mr Hadley the best, and
only, prospect that might come to her.

So it was with some relief that during her stay Margaret noted Mr
Hadley's growing partiality for her. If Margaret and Mrs Fowler
planned a visit to the theatre, Mr Hadley was sure to escort them. If

Margaret had a desire for fresh air, Mr Hadley suggested an excursion to Hampstead. All in all, she did not dislike him. In consequence Mr Hadley spoke, he was accepted, and all that remained was for Mr Shepherd's consent to be granted when he retrieved Margaret at the end of her stay.

Until that time, there was still much of London to delight and amuse them. The evening immediately ahead promised a musical entertainment at the home of some of Mrs Fowler's acquaintances, and it was to have the further benefit of an addition to their party, Captain Cedric Fowler, member of the Royal Horse Guards and Mrs Fowler's brother-in-law. Captain Fowler, Margaret was warned, was a harmless rogue and knew all the best gossip, which made him excessively useful in a gathering of strangers. As the group entered the house in Berkeley Square, Cedric demonstrated this ability by whispering that they could expect to find a genuine adulteress in their midst tonight. Mr Hadley looked shocked, Mrs Fowler said, 'For shame, Cedric,' and Margaret remained silent.

As they sat down, Cedric took in the other occupants in the room and narrowed in on a group gathered near the fireplace. 'Aye, that must be her there,' he pronounced.

'Whom do you mean?' asked Mrs Fowler. 'There are several ladies in that party. The one in the blue silk?'

'No, no, not her. I am sure it is the lady standing for she is tremendously handsome.'

Margaret contemplated the stately woman dressed in an exquisite gown of jonquil and listening attentively to her companion. As the others added their assessment to Cedric's, Margaret found her attention turned to another in the group, a woman who had likely never been called handsome in her life for she had a projecting tooth and took pains to conceal it behind a fan. When she smiled, however, her face lit up a captivating countenance. As Margaret continued to observe her – in truth she could not take her eyes off the lady – her thoughts turned to expression, whispering, 'I believe you are both wrong.'

Mr Hadley followed her gaze and indulged her with a smile. 'I fancy, my dear Miss Clay, that it is rather a good thing that you cannot recognise a lady of ill repute.'

The small band of musicians began to play, and all thought of the adulteress was suspended. The musicians were talented, the room well proportioned, and Margaret lost sight of the lady with the fan until a break in the performance brought about a quest for refreshment by the gentlemen. Margaret, noticing that the lady was exiting the room on the arm of an older man, pleaded an excuse about the fire being too warm and left Mrs Fowler.

Margaret made her way to the landing and could see the couple was already descending the staircase. With only a momentary thought, she reached into her reticule, pulled out a handkerchief, and, taking a few steps forward, heard herself speaking: 'Ma'am, I beg your pardon. You appear to have dropped this.'

She held out the small square of fabric – somewhat faded and frayed – frightened that her courage would fail her if the woman did not turn around. But the woman did, slipping her arm from the gentleman's and joining Margaret on the landing. She studied the handkerchief and then, noticing something, examined Margaret's face.

'How kind of you,' the woman said in a charming voice, taking the handkerchief from Margaret. 'I thank you, Miss…'

'Clay, ma'am,' she replied, a small quiver catching in her throat. 'Margaret Clay.'

It was perceptible for only a moment, but Margaret heard the woman take a short, sharp breath.

'Is this your first visit to London?'

'Yes, ma'am.'

'How do you like it?'

'Oh, very much. I've always wanted to see London. It is very different from Somersetshire.'

'Yes, that it is,' the woman said. 'And what, may I ask, brings you to London?'

Margaret glanced back at the door, shyly. 'I have hopes to…that is, we hope to make an announcement soon.'

23

The woman reached out her gloved hand and touched Margaret gently on the wrist. 'I'm so glad,' she whispered. 'I—'

A cough from further down the stairs prevented any further conversation. The gentleman had now grown impatient. 'Penelope, we really must be off.'

'Of course,' the woman said, gathering the folds of her gown to descend the steps. She looked back at Margaret and was about to say something more when her attention was drawn to Mr Hadley, who was approaching them.

'Miss Clay,' he said, 'the music is about to begin. We mustn't miss it.'

Margaret, her attention diverted for a moment, returned to speak again to the woman but found she was already hurrying down the stairs. Possessed with the same courage she had summoned just before, she leaned against the railing and shouted down: 'I am staying in Portman Square! No. 16.'

'Margaret!' Mr Hadley exclaimed. 'Forgive me, Miss Clay. But have you lost all sense of propriety? What could have possessed you?'

'I…I do not know,' she faltered.

He escorted her toward the door where they were met by Cedric.

'Well,' pronounced Cedric, suppressing a laugh, 'I have winkled out the wolf in sheep's clothing.'

Mr Hadley let out an exasperated sigh. 'Fowler, must you always express yourself in riddles? Speak plainly.'

'If I must. That lady – if I may call her that – fleeing, is the very adulteress we were promised. I have just heard all about her career flitting from one gentleman to another. She once even tried to entice a baronet. She's been married at least twice. One husband dead, though nobody seems to know much about him or his name. The second, however, still lives, but she no longer resides under the conjugal roof, preferring instead the protection of the gentleman with whom she left, an Admiral Lamb.'

'Really, Fowler,' said Mr Hadley, growing impatient and anxiously eyeing Margaret, 'this is hardly suitable talk for Miss Clay's presence.'

'A thousand apologies, my good fellow. And you, ma'am, pray

excuse my coarse manners. I have grown vulgar in the company of my fellow soldiers. But you must allow me to tell you the best part! The lady in question is not so unnatural in trying to secure Admiral Lamb for it seems her maiden name was Shepherd. Have you ever heard the like?' he exclaimed with glee. 'A *shepherd* in search of a *lamb*!'

Margaret would not meet Mr Hadley's eye though she knew he examined her. She could only hope she did not blush too profusely and surprised even herself when she uttered in a calm voice, 'We had better return to our seats.' She did not pause for a response but led the way to where Mrs Fowler waited on a bench. Margaret, focusing all her attention on the musician poised at the harp, did not turn when Mr Hadley took the seat beside her, hissing 'Margaret!' in her ear.

'Thomas, do be quiet,' interjected Mrs Fowler. 'They are starting.'

Mr Hadley reluctantly gave up as the quartet began, but it did not stop him from turning to contemplate Margaret's profile at regular intervals throughout the remainder of the performance. She hoped he did not see the tears that pooled in her eyes, and if they fell down her cheek, she did not wipe them away.

Later, when the carriage was conveying them to Portman Square, the mood was unchanged and little was said amongst the company until Mrs Fowler broke the silence with a laugh saying: 'I fear we are all very dull after an evening of such refined entertainment. You shall have to procure a box for us to see a farce, Thomas, or something else that doesn't put us all into this melancholy state.'

'Perhaps,' said Margaret, speaking for the first time, 'we might finally visit the menagerie at the Tower. I do long to see the tigers.'

'I am afraid I shall have to forgo the pleasure of escorting you both there,' said Mr Hadley. 'Or to the theatre. Urgent business calls me into Lincolnshire in the morning.'

'Urgent business?' asked a perplexed Mrs Fowler. 'But surely you will not stay away long? For, you know, Miss Clay's visit to London is almost at an end.'

'I fear I shall be away for some weeks. I do apologise, Miss Clay.' He spoke with the tone of a gentleman, saying all that was correct. Margaret did not fear to meet his eye now.

'I perfectly understand, Mr Hadley,' she said. 'You must do what you know to be right.'

By then they had reached No. 16, and Mr Hadley, who usually gave himself the privilege of helping Miss Clay alight from the carriage, allowed the footman to do his regular duty. He left them a few moments later, staying only long enough to bid the ladies a good night and to wish Miss Clay a pleasant time for the remainder of her stay in London. His sister watched his departure in astonishment, and after they had divested themselves of cloaks and gloves, she ushered Miss Clay upstairs into the drawing room for some sort of explanation.

'Have you quarrelled, my dear Margaret?' she asked.

'Not that I am aware,' Margaret returned. 'We did not have much conversation this evening.'

'But are you not alarmed at this change, or the way he took his leave of us just now?'

'I am sure Mr Hadley expressed himself properly. Why should I merit a goodbye any different? You are his sister. I am nothing to him.'

'Nothing? You call yourself nothing?' She regarded her friend sitting composedly before the fire. 'But he—'

'Better we know ourselves now than later,' Margaret said, staring into the flames momentarily before standing up. 'Pray excuse me, but I very much wish to go to sleep.'

Mrs Fowler was about to deny this request and press her with further questions, but a sober resolve reflected in Margaret's eyes that could not be contradicted. She was allowed to slip away to her bedchamber as she liked, but the wish for sleep did not follow.

The next day, Margaret declined an invitation to join Mrs Fowler on her morning calls and soon found herself mistress of the drawing room with an uncut volume from the latest Waverly novel to while away the hours. Taking a seat near the window so as to command a view of the street below, she looked amusedly at the title she held in her hands – *The Betrothed* – and while trying not to listen for the sounds of a carriage rattling over the cobblestones, she managed to be drawn into the tale of Welsh feuds of the late twelfth century.

So absorbed was she in the plight of young Eveline that a knock on the door and the entrance of a footman surprised her. The small parcel he presented to her before quitting the room was even more astonishing. It was wrapped up in simple brown paper and tied with twine. Untying it, her eyes were first arrested by a neat but faded cambric handkerchief with a design of ivy leaves encircling the embroidered initials 'PS'. Margaret held the familiar fabric in her hands, tracing the letters with her finger, and only then noticed the piece of paper that lay between its folds. It read:

I return to you the handkerchief that has been so thoughtfully preserved all these years. Little did I think I should ever see it again. There is much I would like to say, but please do not be so foolish as to wish to know me. I have no desire to jeopardise your future happiness, and any intimacy between us would do just that. You may choose to believe me or not, but I did first leave you with the best of intentions. I soon learned, however, that trying to secure a home and a better future do not always bring one happiness. If I have any right to offer you advice, let it be this: do not live a life of regret. Accept the decisions you make and learn from them. No good comes from being consumed by disappointment.

May God bless you, my dear.

Margaret sat staring at the unsigned note for some time. A bustling noise in the corridor told her Mrs Fowler had returned from her calls, so she hastily inserted the note into the pages of her book. As she was about to close the volume, her eyes fell on a passage that seemed to Margaret to be an act of Providence:

'Now all ye ladies of fair Scotland,
And ladies of England that happy would prove,
Marry never for houses, nor marry for land
Nor marry for nothing but only love.'

A THING OF BEAUTY

Sarah Baillie

As she alighted from the carriage and took in the scene before her – one of well-dressed ladies and gentlemen flitting through the December gloom into the warmth of Admiral Corrigan's reception rooms – Mrs Godolphin reflected upon the joy a little coloured silk can bring. The year now nearing its end had been one of dark shades, the rustling of black crepe ever present. Barely a month had passed after the people of England had lightened the colours of their mourning for poor Princess Charlotte, before Mrs Godolphin and her family were again enveloped in deepest black. The veil was this time drawn across her attractive face to mask the pain of a more personal loss – that of her dear brother-in-law, the Colonel.

It had been a long year of letters and visits, of endless nights holding her bereft sister and of comforting the children. These duties thus fulfilled, Mrs Godolphin felt that her path now lay in bringing her sister's family to life once more. At her urging, Captain Godolphin had entered into a correspondence with young Charles, her nephew, offering his counsel on the management of the estate. Although the Godolphins themselves did not own land, they were very well-connected with the loftier branches of the Captain's family and did in fact enjoy establishments both at port and in town. It was therefore to be hoped that, should Charles require an experienced steward, one might be easily procured through the Captain's connections.

Having lost her own father at an early juncture, and with two older sisters who were both too mature to provide much distraction at the time, Mrs Godolphin now felt the great importance of entertainment for the younger nieces and nephews. This was being gladly supplied by their other aunt, whose home lay within the grounds of the estate, and whose own sons were at their studies in Oxford.

This left only the eldest, Caroline, for whom Mrs Godolphin had decided to take responsibility; her mother remaining in full mourning. Her eighteenth birthday having recently passed, and the period of mourning finally at an end, it was, her aunts and mother believed, full time for Caroline to enter society.

Turning to assist her niece from the carriage, Mrs Godolphin was struck anew by the change that the last year had wrought in Caroline's face. A snowdrop in a stormy winter, Caroline had blossomed despite grief and responsibility. Her height, previously rather cumbersome in a girl of seventeen, had become elegant in womanhood. Her step was light, her smile easy, and her eyes a lively brown. Beneath a gauzy black veil, Caroline had become the very picture of her mother at the same age.

As the two ladies made their way into the house, Mrs Godolphin was silently grateful for Lady Corrigan's attention to the fireplaces, and to her liberal use of invitation cards. Having wed a naval officer both for love and in the hope of exploring the wider world that she had discovered as a child in her father's library, Mrs Godolphin had thought herself truly fortunate to spend some years in the swelter of the West Indies. The result of this sojourn, however, was that Mrs Godolphin had grown vastly intolerant of the English winter. Thankfully, tonight, Lady Corrigan's ballroom was warm, bright, and thronging with people. Familiar faces abounded, and Mrs Godolphin felt quite at her ease; even with her husband away, she should be able to introduce her niece to many new acquaintances by the end of the evening.

'Come, Caroline, dear,' said Mrs Godolphin, beckoning. 'I see Captain and Mrs Howard standing nearby.'

Caroline had not taken two steps before, jostled by the crowd, a young lady fell upon her and stepped onto the hem of Caroline's gown. With a faint tearing sound, two of the delicate lace scallops came away, and the woman blushed with apologies. Mrs Godolphin hurried to Caroline's assistance, but was gently dismissed; the innocent perpetrator, introduced as one Mrs Farraway, could help Caroline to hide the damage, and they would return immediately. Mrs Godolphin smiled as they darted away, becoming immediate friends in that easy way most particular to young ladies. Turning to find Mrs Howard again, Mrs Godolphin found her gaze arrested by a face at the edge of the dance. Perhaps she had been thinking too much of the days of her youth…for this was a face she had known only too well as a child. The jaw was perhaps a little less defined, the complexion somewhat dimmed, but the countenance of the man before her was no less handsome than the day he had first come to her mother's home, carrying her elder sister in his arms.

After a moment's hesitation, during which the gentleman's expressive grey eyes had glanced her way, Mrs Godolphin made up her mind to turn away, to pretend that she had not seen him. She had been too young quite to comprehend what had passed between that gentleman and her family, but she knew that there had for a time been a great deal of tears – some of them her own. She had once liked him very much, and had been greatly disappointed by his disappearance from her life, but was placated by her sister's alternative choice of husband. It was better by far to avoid the man. But, too late! He was there before her, bowing his head and regarding her quizzically.

'Madam,' he said, smiling. 'I beg you to forgive my impertinence; I am sure that I recognise you, but cannot quite recall your name. Is your husband among my acquaintance?'

'I believe Captain Godolphin has never had the pleasure of your company, Mr Willoughby,' she replied. 'But I have, indeed – in Devon, many years ago.'

The grey eyes grew wide with surprise, and darted quickly from side to side. Mrs Godolphin wondered if Mr Willoughby was afraid to be overheard – or seeking escape. After a moment he gathered himself.

'Miss Margaret Dashwood?' he cried with delight, stepping nearer. 'What a great and unexpected pleasure to see you, indeed!'

Margaret allowed him to shake her hand, unsure of how to proceed. Mr Willoughby did not seem to notice her hesitation; rather, fascination shone in his eyes. The expression seemed to melt away the years, and once again he was a man of five-and-twenty, and Margaret felt in some danger of becoming the awkward fifteen-year-old who had so greatly admired him, and wished for him to become her brother.

'You are well, I hope?' Mr Willoughby inquired. 'And your family?'

'I am quite well, thank you. My husband and sons are in Portsmouth, and I have brought my niece to town for the season. She is recently out of mourning, you see, and in need of distraction.'

Mr Willoughby gave a slight start at this, and his brow furrowed in concern. 'I am sorry to hear that. May I enquire as to…' He faltered. 'How did your niece come to be in mourning?'

'Oh!' Margaret realised the cause of Mr Willoughby's discomfort. 'My mother and sisters are all very well…'

Mr Willoughby nodded and said politely that he was glad to hear it, as if he had not moments previously appeared quite pale at his quick imaginings.

'No,' Margaret continued, sadly, 'It is my dear brother, Colonel Brandon, who has died.'

At this, Margaret suddenly found that she could not read Willoughby's expression, for his mind seemed to have gone elsewhere. She wondered again how little she truly knew of all that had passed between Willoughby and Marianne. As time had passed and her understanding of relationships, loyalties and frailties had increased a little, Margaret had guessed at some of it, but Marianne had been so settled in her life with the Colonel that Margaret had not wanted to disturb her sister's contentment with questions.

'I beg you will convey my condolences to Mrs Brandon,' said Mr Willoughby, finally.

Margaret thought of Marianne's sorrow, of the fragile peace and serenity that the three sisters had forged at Delaford over the past year. Could she possibly disturb it now with unsolicited condolences from a man whose name had not been uttered in that house for many years? She felt sure that she could not, could almost hear Elinor's calm voice warning her to extricate herself from this situation.

'I—' she began, but was interrupted.

'I myself was widowed three years ago,' Mr Willoughby continued. 'Perhaps I understand, as I believe I once did, some of what your dear sister feels.'

Margaret felt heat rise in her cheeks, but whether this was due to shock or anger at his presumption, and what might have been her reply, was never to be answered, for at that moment she heard Caroline's voice behind her.

Mr Willoughby's eyes moved past Margaret, and he seemed to turn to stone, his elegant features suddenly captured in marble. The colour drained from his face, and all his charm and ease seemed to have quite abandoned him. Margaret felt that she was witnessing a haunting amidst a bright, jumbling ballroom. Turning, she saw what had so affected Mr Willoughby. A spectre had indeed risen up before him; her niece, so lovely, so innocent and quite unaffected, was now moving through the ballroom. There were times when Margaret looked at her little sons, and saw the men they would become. She saw her husband's intelligence in Henry's brow, saw her own thirst for adventure on John's scraped knees. And now she looked at Caroline, and beheld exactly what had so thoroughly changed Willoughby's countenance. Through her eldest daughter's face, Marianne before illness, disappointment or grief had ever touched her was smiling freely at them both, with no idea of what they saw or felt.

'I apologise for my absence, Aunt,' beamed Caroline. 'As you can see, my new friend Mrs Farraway has hidden talents!'

She flicked the hem of her skirt with a heel, making the lace scallops flutter. Receiving no reply, Caroline looked curiously from her aunt to the stranger by her side.

Margaret gently placed a hand on Caroline's arm. 'Mr Willoughby, allow me to introduce my niece, Miss Caroline Brandon.'

Caroline gave a small curtsy, and sent her aunt a questioning look. Margaret had no choice but to continue the introduction.

'Mr Willoughby is a former acquaintance of the family,' she said, hoping to curb Caroline's curiosity. However, this was not to be, for Mr Willoughby himself intervened.

'I was a particular friend of your mother's, Miss Brandon,' he said, smiling at her surprise. 'I do hope that you will remember me to her when you next write.'

'But of course I will! How wonderful,' exclaimed Caroline. 'I am sure it will cheer her to hear from an old friend.'

'An old friend indeed, but not, I hope, an elderly friend,' Mr Willoughby replied, his charm seemingly restored by Caroline's enthusiasm.

As her niece laughed, Margaret began to cast about for a nearby acquaintance to whom she could introduce Caroline quickly, and put an end to whatever was happening before her. Again, Margaret felt that she could not quite comprehend the workings of Mr Willoughby's mind, but now age and experience told her that whatever it was ought not come to fruition. Beyond the dancing couples, she again spotted Captain Howard and his wife, and tried to catch her friend's eye. However, she was thwarted in this endeavour by the figure of a young man stepping into her path.

He was tall, and of slender but strong build. Dark hair curled around his collar, and as he began to apologise for obstructing her view, Margaret looked up to see a pair of familiar grey eyes set above high cheekbones.

'Ah,' said Mr Willoughby, reluctantly drawing his attention from Caroline's laughing face. 'Mrs Godolphin, Miss Brandon, please allow me to present my son, Jack.'

The young man joined the group, and nodded at Margaret and Caroline, his face bright and open. 'It is a pleasure to meet you both. And may I say how pleasant it is to find that my father has once again found and engaged in conversation the most delightful ladies present at a gathering.'

Caroline did not appear to notice the sharp look sent from father to son, so occupied was she with the latter's compliments towards her appearance.

'I am afraid, Mr Willoughby,' said she, 'that this is not my newest gown, and that it will be quite unfashionable before the year is out.'

Margaret began to chide Caroline for speaking so openly, but found herself interrupted.

'Nonsense, Miss Brandon!' Jack Willoughby exclaimed. '"*A thing of beauty is a joy forever.*"'

'But that is Keats!' replied Caroline, laughing.

The interest in young Willoughby's eyes increased, and he inclined his head towards the young lady. 'Do you know *Endymion* then, Miss Brandon?'

'My mother has read it a good deal these past months. She is a great lover of poetry, and I must confess to sharing her tastes.'

The elder Mr Willoughby's mouth quirked into an arresting smile. 'It pleases me to hear that Mrs Brandon has found comfort in poetry. 'Twas ever her way.'

Margaret felt the danger of the situation increasing, and although she was a woman grown, both capable and clever, she wished she could briefly be again an ineffectual, irresponsible child. She did not fully understand the dance taking place before her, could not predict the movements of the participants.

'Indeed,' added Mr Willoughby, 'I feel that Cynthia's words on reuniting with Endymion might appeal to Mrs Brandon's sensibilities, at least as I once knew her.'

Caroline blushed a little as she confessed that the poem was of such length that she had really only memorised the first hundred lines or so. Jack Willoughby was charmed, but his father was intense.

'The lines I refer to are: "But now of all the world I love thee best. There is not one, no, no, not one but thee."' Mr Willoughby avoided Margaret's gaze as he spoke, and watched with pleasure as Caroline took in his words.

'I thank you sir; I do believe those lines would bring my mother great comfort,' she said thoughtfully. 'She did love my father so.'

Mr Willoughby's smile did not falter, but Margaret saw his jaw stiffen.

'An admirable sentiment indeed,' said Jack Willoughby. 'And now, enough of poetry. What of music?'

Margaret watched as her niece was engaged to dance by the son of Mr Willoughby and knew that the attraction between the young pair was not merely of her imagining. Mr Willoughby stood silently by her side, his jaw still twitching. The lines he had recited echoed in Margaret's mind, and she began to feel that the tumult of the past year was not yet over. She would have to write to Elinor...

FORGOTTEN THINGS

Emily Ruth Verona

No Breath of air to break the wave
That rolls below the Athenian's grave,
That tomb which, gleaming o'er the cliff,
First greets the homeward-veering skiff,
High o'er the land he saved in vain;
When shall such hero live again?

The Giaour by Lord Byron

James couldn't breathe. The air hung in the back of his throat, swollen and unforgiving. He felt stifled by the height of the bridge and the heaviness of his feet beneath him. This had been building surely, it had started just nearly a month ago but the force of it was overpowering. The distortion of detail. The slipping of facts.

In the beginning, grief had been the sole comfort to his quiet disposition. It was his crutch, his companion, his one true, twisted love. He'd relied on grief and all that it brought to him: the ways in which it preserved the memory of her. Grief allowed him to cling to the sweetness of Fanny's face, her eyes, in particular, which glowed even when the silence between them was almost too much to bear. The mark on her neck, there from the day of her birth to that of her death. The floury softness of her hair. The stern curve of her lip. Only now…he could no longer recall the precise colour of those glowing eyes, nor the side of her neck on which the mark resided. Her hair had been golden surely, but whether it was a golden brown or a wheatly yellow he could not say. He should have known these things. He was the bearer of her loss. The keeper of her subtleties. It was his responsibility to remember her. All of her. It was within him now that her life resided. And without the feeling of her presence he no longer knew her. And if he did not know her, then the mysteries of his own self were forever lost to him.

Even with the absence of air in his lungs James edged himself forward, tipping his head over the water. It was black as oil beneath him and distantly he could hear infant waves knocking against the base of the bridge. He almost found it comforting to stand there under the moonlit, starless sky. He opened his mouth slightly in the hope that a sip of air might revive him, but his lips only felt the frost of the evening and bitterness of the wind.

He gripped the railing with his numbing palms and stretched his body out, tight against the pull of his arms. He felt himself sway and sway and he could almost see her. With his eyes closed and his focus trained he could almost see her face, but it was only *almost*, and *nearly* was sure to follow, and then *vaguely*, until the day would come when he could barely even remember that face. What life was that? What purpose lies in a world that could so easily let slip those things most precious to his heart? None, of course. There was no purpose at all without Fanny, no guiding course. After all, she was the one in his life to reside closest to the bone. Her name was all but carved along his ribs and yet there he stood unable to remember the placement of that mark on her neck. The colour of her hair. The look of her eyes.

Slowly James pulled himself back, his shoulders low and rigid. He opened his eyes and stared out along the emptiness. Far off he could hear cars and streets and life, but from where he stood it was quiet. From where he stood it was good.

He closed his eyes again and slipped a hand into the pocket of his jeans. When it turned out empty he felt around in the other, but what he was looking for wasn't there either. He opened his eyes. Checked his jacket carefully, moving through each pocket one by one. He couldn't have…after everything he couldn't have misplaced…only it wasn't there. Like everything else, he had forgotten it. The lighter Fanny had given him. It was still sitting on the counter in his apartment and without it he realised he felt even emptier than before. He rechecked his pockets a second and third time only to come to the same result. What should he do? Go home and bring it back here? He could not imagine making this walk again, nor wasting another moment apart from her. Still he hesitated, as if she would not recognise him in the afterlife without it, as if it were the beacon that would once again draw them together.

'Are you going to jump?'

The voice nearly startled him right off the edge. He turned his stiff neck to see a young woman standing by the rail, her hands in her pockets and her lower lip tucked inward. She was dressed for nowhere in particularly, a long, large coat buttoned up to her neck.

'No,' he replied before looking back out onto the water.

'Then why are you standing on that side?'

'Because.'

'You're going to jump,' she insisted, uncomfortably.

'No I'm not, now go away.'

She remained motionless.

'Go,' he urged her.

The girl stared at him plainly. 'I don't want to.'

'Why not?'

'Look at you.'

He stopped, trying to avoid her gaze until at last it proved to be too much for him. He glanced up, her dark features darker still in the night. He had seen her before, with Fred or maybe Anne at a party or a restaurant or one of those grotesquely inane events they'd all dragged him to. Hoping they would breathe some life into him. Hoping they would revive his stalling heart. Only they hadn't been capable of it, as desperately as they'd tried. For the longest time a darkness had been hovering, slowly making its way beneath his skin, through the veins. That darkness circulated through him like a poison. It fed his thoughts. Fuelled his impulses. It had become a part of him, or maybe even it had been there all along, waiting for the day to come when Fanny would not be there to comfort him.

This girl didn't seem to recognise him though and in spite of everything he was thankful for it. He did not need her to know him. Understand him. He just needed her to leave, if only she would. 'Can I help you with something?' he asked, impatiently.

'I'd rather you not, if you don't mind,' she said.

'Not what?'

'Jump.'

He stared at her, noting the hopeful gleam of her expression behind the matter-of-fact way in which she spoke the words. 'It would be an awful thing.'

He squinted irritably. 'Would it really?'

'Yes,' she replied with alarming decisiveness. 'It would.'

'Maybe I already did it.' He smiled, cynically. 'Maybe this is death.'

'I doubt it,' said the girl.

'And why is that?'

'Because heaven isn't an empty bridge in the middle of the night.'

'Then maybe this is hell.'

She tilted her head softly to the side. 'Do I look like I'm in hell?'

'You're too pretty for hell,' he admitted, hating himself almost immediately after saying it. Imagining the way Fanny would hate him for having said it.

She smiled with more modesty than he would have thought her capable of possessing. If this was going to be his last earthly conversation, then at least it would not be a boring one.

'Thank you,' she said.

'Yet, maybe that's the point,' he added, dryly.

'Excuse me?'

'Hell is probably filled with pretty girls.'

'Or maybe this is your hell,' she offered in response, 'The personal kind. One that's real. The sort populated by unhappy people.'

'I'm not unhappy.'

'You're leaning off a bridge.'

'I'm not leaning.'

'Well you're more off than on I would say.'

James looked back at the water. 'Just go away,' he muttered.

'So you can jump?'

'I told you, I'm not going to jump.'

'Then why are you on that side of the rail?'

'Are we going to do this all night?' he barked.

The girl jumped, startled by the fierceness of his bite. He was more the wounded animal than she'd realised. 'I've met you before,' she whispered suddenly, slowly piecing together the features of his face even in the dark. 'You're James Benwick—'

'No…'

'You knew that girl—'

'No…'

'The one who died.'

'Shut up,' he continued, steadily, though underneath the words the strings that held him to civility were beginning to snap one by one.

'I'm sorry you're going through this—'

'Shut up!' he insisted with more force than was warranted and less than he had actually intended. He wanted to sound brutal. Monstrous. Unforgiving. He wanted to lash out in all the ways he had never known how to lash out before. Beyond his mild manner. Beyond his quiet countenance. He wanted to find himself capable of the most pure, cruel hate.

The girl frowned. 'It must be terrible to—'

Just stop it!' he shouted.

He swung at her, only in doing so his foot slipped and his footing stumbled. For a moment he was falling. The first full breath to grace his lips in over an hour came rushing down his throat and as his fingers scrambled to grab something he choked and cried and tried even to swear himself through it. He grabbed the railing, pulling himself up and hugging his chest tightly against it, trying to spit the breath back out again, but it had already woken the dormant air that lay at the bottom of his lungs. He took one icy, deep breath after another and another and another. The addiction of it was intoxicating. He felt lightheaded and cowardly and alive. When he looked up again the girl was standing right above him, her fingers along the rail only inches from his own. He looked into her eyes, her deep, dark, endless eyes that frightened him more than the sky or the water or the fact that he could no longer bear to look over the edge.

The girl didn't say anything, and there was no pity in her stare. No resentment. Disdain. Or disgust. She edged her fingers just a bit closer to his. And he let her. 'Can I stay here a while?' she asked at last.

He almost couldn't find a response. 'W…why?' he whispered.

'Because I want to,' she said. Quietly she slipped her fingers across his knuckles. They were warmer than he remembered skin ever being.

With her forefinger and her thumb she shook his index finger gently. 'Louisa.'

He could only look at her, struggling to find even his own name. And then when he did, it barely even sounded like a word he remembered ever saying before. In fact, it didn't feel like his name. He wanted it to belong to someone else. A stranger. Someone more alive. 'James,' he muttered shakily.

They stood there like that, his arms seemingly tied in knots around the railing and her fingers like tethers between him and this world. Neither said a word for a minute, then two, then five. They stood in silence as the moon shifted in the sky and his fingers started to warm again beneath the care of her own.

Then, just as it seemed like the silence would last into eternity, she frowned with quiet fear. 'Don't jump,' she said again.

He thought of that lighter in his apartment. He felt the weight of Fanny's heart in his own, the distance of her memory and the pain of her absence in his chest. He needed her eyes. Her hair. Her neck. Her lips. All of it. All of her. She had been buried deep inside his heart and to remove that weight would be to leave a hole gaping in his chest. He just couldn't stand to let go of her.

'I won't,' he said, suddenly. Only this time, unlike the times before, he meant it.

ALL AT SEA

Sandy Norris

Captain Frederick Wentworth, resplendent in his new blue frock coat and gold lace, stood on the quarterdeck of his command and surveyed the busy scene along the length of the ship, where his men were working. High above the deck, a number of able seamen were stretched along the cross-trees to the main mast, lacing on the new sail. On deck, and close by, a gang of seamen – the unskilled and conscripted – were spread across the deck amidships on their knees holystoning the planking. He was not a feared captain as some were, so that his appearance now did little to lessen the low-level banter amongst them. Nevertheless, it was in his hands, on his word that a recalcitrant worker might be flogged at the grating in the name of discipline and good order.

Moored off Portsmouth Harbour and pulling against her anchor cable, while the tide ebbed, the ship was being readied for her imminent departure. Captain Wentworth balanced as easily as if he were on dry land. After all those months on land between commissions and between wars, he was back where he was most at ease. The ship was well-positioned, easily within reach of the land, so that the repairs needed from their last action had been carried out with little difficulty, but for anyone wishing to board, the only way onto his world was by passage in the ship's boat and this now threatened to spoil his joy.

Having recently assumed the enviable position of being a man married to the lady he loved and who sincerely loved him back, he should have been happy, yet his brow was furrowed. His dearest, loveliest Anne – Mrs Anne Wentworth, to use her new title – had lived all her life on dry land, immured, for the most of it, in a tiny village in the confines of what he was pleased teasingly to call the 'sprigged muslin' routine of life. But now she was to join him at sea. And the more he cast his mind around the variety of unladylike parts and actions of the ship, the more he doubted the wisdom of his acceding to her wish to follow him wherever he went across the world. He should have been strong and settled her safely in their new house, close to his family home in the village of…

The bell clanged to change the watch and he stood calmly, anxiety hidden, watching his crew appearing and disappearing according to the section leaders' commands. With Napoleon escaped from Elba and leading a new army, it would not be more than a day or two before they set sail. His orders had yet to arrive, but when they did he was sure they would command him to head once more for Gibraltar and to blockade the southern ports. And the chances of a sea battle would be high.

In all her life Anne had probably never set sail in a boat of any kind. He turned swiftly, saluted the sentry on guard outside his cabin, ducked his head to avoid the low lintel with the same automatic reflex that he used to breathe and re-entered his quarters. The Great Cabin stretched right across the stern of the ship. When he thought back to the lieutenant's hutch he had shared, watch-on watch-off, with Kingsley, where there was just enough room to stow their trunks under the bunk, this was a palace, his sanctuary away from the rest of the ship. But to Anne, used to the space of Kellynch Hall or the family's lodgings in Bath, it must surely seem like a prison cell.

Before Anne, he had vowed never to have a woman on board, but the thought of parting so soon after their wedding, added to the strength of her pleading, had led to his surrender and she was on her way. She would at this moment be riding in the carriage loaned to her by Admiral Croft, so that she could be ferried across the harbour.

'If you please, Sir…'

The Captain turned to see his servant, Andrews.

'Yes, John, what is it?'

'I have been thinking, Sir. What with Mrs Wentworth coming aboard…' The man, small in stature but swift of mind stood firm on the deck. 'Sir, if we were to run a curtain on the starboard side, she could have that as her dressing room, Sir.'

Captain Wentworth paused, viewed the suggested changes and smiled.

'What would I do without you, Andrews? See to it directly.'

He turned again to look through the stern lights and shuddered. During the voyage Anne could stay here with reasonable comfort, if no variety, but that would disappear when the enemy were sighted.

And what when they were embroiled in battle? In battle, all privacy and safety disappeared. All screens were torn down and stowed. This would become part of the deck. His eye rested on the two covered mounds on either side of the cabin. Beneath the velvet covers were guns, ready to be used in anger against the French.

He pictured her as he last saw her, with her neat pink bonnet, white ruffled collar just peeping out from the neck of her equally neat pink dress. He glanced at the upright padded chair sent abroad by his friend Admiral Croft, specifically for Anne's use and the solid oak card table constructed by Timms, the ship's carpenter, using left over lengths from his other tasks, in honour of their marriage. A gesture that had quite overwhelmed him, suggesting as it did that the crew generally revered him. Would this be enough?

Then a shout from on deck forced him to bring his mind back to the present. He re-settled his hat and strode on deck where his first lieutenant and best friend, Charles Knight, stood by the shrouds. 'Captain, you might want to use this,' he said, smiling. 'I believe your lady is on her way.' He handed over the ship's main telescope and Captain Wentworth extended the mahogany tube and raised it to his eye.

After a few seconds he homed in on the jetty at Portsmouth Hard, lowered the glass slightly and located the ship's boat where, sitting quite calmly facing the bank of oarsmen, he saw his wife in miniature. He held the glass steady and peered through it until his eye watered, watching as the small boat grew larger, noting how smartly turned out were his crew in her honour. His wife!

The boat drew nearer and he watched Anne's face, now he could make out her features. He watched as she studied his ship, her expression showing a keen interest. Standing on his left, his friend sighed. 'You are lucky, Sir, to have found such a companion.'

Captain Wentworth turned. 'Did I tell you how my stubborn nature almost caused me to lose her? How with a little persuasion on my part, we could have been married these last seven years?'

The lieutenant raised an eyebrow.

'Mrs Wentworth has too low an opinion of herself and was

persuaded, being at the time still very young, that it would be beneath her to accept my proposals. But I can think of no one more capable of putting up with my whims than she. She is unflappable and quite calm in any emergency. Had I not been possessed with too much stupid pride I would have won the day, but instead I removed myself and sulked.'

'And now you have your fortune and have renewed your interest and her family are all in favour of the connection, I surmise.'

'Sir you are too astute,' he smiled, 'but it is to my gain.' Then he stepped over to where the side party had fallen in, ready to welcome Mrs Wentworth to their world.

And here she was, in a simple blue bonnet and dark blue velvet cape over her plain grey gown, being hoist aboard in the bosun chair looking for all the world as though she was subject to this undignified mode of transport every day of her life. His heart beat faster and he took her arm as she stepped onto the deck, the move being well-timed as a gust of wind whisked her cape to one side so that she lost balance, unused to the shifting ground.

She stood swaying gently as she looked around so that he felt compelled to place a restraining hand in the small of her back. Then he became aware of an unusual silence surrounding them and looking about realised that the whole crew had gathered to see her; there was no inch of spare space left. All caps had been removed and the men and boys were crowded around to meet their Captain's lady.

Anne hardly seemed flustered. She turned her face up to him and smiled. 'Frederick, you must show me every corner of your ship. This is my home as much as it is yours, now, and I want to know it all.'

First Lieutenant Charles Knight called for three cheers for the Captain's lady. The roar of rough voices might have overwhelmed any lady but Anne. She smiled and stood her ground. Captain Wentworth thanked them on her behalf, bidding them return to their tasks and by the end of ten minutes the deck was clear and the two of them were left in peace.

The Captain led his lady along the deck so that she might feel the air in the bows, see how the ship tapered towards its prow and stood proud above the water. But while they walked, his mind was busy with below decks. How could she be exposed to the gun deck where the common seamen ate, slept and spent their leisure, where in rough weather they were kennelled like dogs and shut away from daylight for hours on end? And this was better than the orlop deck below, with its strange smells rising from the ship's bilges and its barrels of stores where the rats scampered to feast. Captain Wentworth shuddered and while Anne paused to look back across the ship's side towards the harbour, he castigated himself again for allowing this to happen.

While they were at supper a wind blew up so that the ship canted awkwardly on her tether. The Captain watched his wife's face, imagined he saw some measure of uncertainty and did his best to keep the conversation light. His orders had arrived by courier brig and they were to sail on the morning tide. For their first evening together, last evening near land, he had invited Charles Knight to join them and also the Surgeon – Edward Simpson, an intelligent educated man with a social conscience that had made him sign on to a life at sea in order to improve the lot of those conscripted into serving their country. With relief he saw how Anne was much engaged with this idea and that future meals might allow such friendships to grow. The evening, he was pleased to admit, was a success.

The morning brought more wind and although his First Lieutenant did an efficient job of readying the ship, Captain Wentworth felt obliged to be present on deck, so that Anne was left to sort for herself. As the daylight grew a watery sun appeared in the ragged windswept sky and he noticed that far from staying below, she had found (or maybe John Andrews had found for her) an officer's heavy boat cloak and she climbed the steps to his quarterdeck and took her place at his side.

He was just about to advise her not to stay long and catch a chill when there was a sudden shout and seconds later a dull thud. He swung his gaze across the width of the deck. Somebody had fallen. Yes, there he was. He watched in concern as a handful of men crowded round to help. When he turned to tell Anne what was amiss, however, all he found was the space she had vacated. And then he saw her hurrying from the bottom of the steps straight to where the body of the man lay. He didn't know what to do, felt helpless for all his invested authority. But he made himself watch her moves and unexpectedly, found his mind back on the walk along the Cobb at Lime. He lived again through his growing admiration as she had taken control after Louisa Musgrove's accident; issued quiet sensible commands for Captain Brodick – not himself – to fetch a surgeon, as he had local knowledge. Then it dawned on him. Anne might actually be happy here.

He remembered how all the time he had known her she had wanted to be useful. She had wanted to live her life being sensible and in the company of other intelligent people. On board, he now saw, she could be busy and purposeful and the crew would be the more settled. The surgeon now appeared to order the transfer of the injured man down to his operating deck and Anne followed.

In the following hour, the anchor was hove short, all men arranged in their places ready to hoist sail as the ship turned into wind. Anne reappeared wearing a large apron, her eyes sparkling. The order was given, the anchor brought up and the vessel lunged like some wild beast, steadied and began her passage towards the open sea. Captain Wentworth took up his usual pose, just ahead of the mizzen mast, so that most of the crew could see him and his wife stood gallantly at his side. To port, the Needles of the Isle of Wight grew closer and slid by, while to starboard, Hurst Castle loomed, its guns brilliant in the new morning sun.

MARY CRAWFORD'S LAST LETTER

Elisabeth Lenckos

Dear Fanny Price,

Or as I should call you now, Lady Bertram – since Edmund and you have outlived Sir Thomas and the heir apparent. How fortunate for you both that Tom never married. I, of course, knew he never would, given I once caught him with Mr Yates. O, the stories I could tell about the Bertram family. You never credited me enough for my discretion.

How does it feel to be mistress of Mansfield Park? Are you in control of the servants? And does your conscience rest more easily, now that Edmund has sold the plantation in the West Indies to a gentleman of less tender feelings than himself? I wonder, did the proceeds from the sale go to a good cause, or did you use them for improvements on the house? How fare the children? Or is it still only the one offspring? I can never remember whether you had a boy or a girl.

I can't imagine Edmund still gives sermons. The management of Mansfield Park must take up all his time. When he has business in London, do you allow him to travel on his own? Or are you afraid he will find himself a mistress, a lively, full-blooded female who conforms to his ideal of beauty, such as I once did? Tell me, are you still frail and brittle, or have you filled out since I saw you last?

Has Mrs Rushworth been welcomed back to Mansfield Park? Or do you insist she remains in exile? Do you ever think of Henry, my brother, with whom she eloped? And do you still pretend that you never took an interest yourself? *O, what a Henry!* Why could you never see that men such as he should be indulged? Look at the dullards most women have to endure, and then be so honest as to admit that you too, were smitten, by his charm, his beauty, and his wit.

So what if he was a flirt? His making love to you must have been the most exciting adventure you ever experienced in your attic-bound life. If only you had a little more courage, you could have been the wife of the most handsome, clever man who ever breathed. What a fine painting by Reynolds or Lawrence the four of us would have made, 'The Bertram-Crawford Families at Mansfield Park.' The artist could have depicted us elegantly grouped; I, playing my harp, Henry, reading his Shakespeare, Edmund and you, gazing admiringly upon the siblings who brought such taste and refinement into your world.

For you were meant to be a spectator, Fanny Price, you were not born to shine. It was I who took you from backstage and put you centre, but instead of being grateful you secretly revised the play I had written for my stay at Mansfield Park. I called it 'Mary,' about a young woman who fled the corruption of the metropolis to find peace and serenity on a remote country estate. Cultured and accomplished, she could not help bewitching its heir who, after a lightning courtship, laid his heart and considerable fortune at her feet.

Or so I hoped and dreamt. However, Master Tom was away from Mansfield Park when I arrived, and I had to make do with his younger brother, Edmund, who immediately fell in love with me. Hoping to make his older sibling jealous, I welcomed his attentions, but when Tom finally put in an appearance, he had a surprise in store for me. He showed no interest in the female sex. Instead, he was devoted to the theatre – the theatre and Mr Yates.

How clever of the young men to put on their amateur theatrical, *Lovers' Vows*, so as to detract attention away from their attachment. They fooled the Bertrams, but not me. As I watched them acting out their passion, I realised that if I wanted to remain at Mansfield Park, I had better make sure of Edmund. Of course, I wished that Tom could be got out of the way, and when news came of his illness, I was, for a while, unable to believe my luck. If he died, I thought, his younger brother would make the perfect husband – landed, rich, and utterly devoted to me.

Why, Fanny Price, did you have to unravel my plot? Not that I ever thought you a worthy rival, but you were supposed to stay in Portsmouth, where Sir Thomas had banished you. Instead, you came back to Mansfield Park at the height of the crisis and nursed the eldest son back to health. How could the Bertrams help but be grateful? Really, Fanny, you practically forced Edmund to propose to you. Tell me – were you not ashamed to accept his offer of marriage, knowing that his passion for me still burnt brightly? Or did you enjoy suffocating the flame of his infatuation with the cold breath of your virtue and chastity?

Why would you not take my brother – Henry who pursued you so ardently? By spurning him, you drove him into the arms of Maria

Rushworth. You, and you alone, are to blame for his fall into sin. Did you never wonder why he abandoned Maria? Why their attachment did not last? You thought him a libertine, but you were wrong. He left your cousin not because he grew tired of her, but to be with me. He always was the most loyal of men.

'The hypocrite,' he cried when I told him that Edmund had slighted me. 'I will challenge him to a duel.'

'You will not,' I commanded him. 'What if Edmund wounds and kills *you*? We must come up with a better way of evening the score.'

I thought for a moment. 'You must jilt Maria. Without you by her side, she will not be received back into society, and her family's reputation will be ruined. Neither Julia nor Fanny will then be able to find husbands.'

Henry stared at me. 'That is ingenious, sister, and may I say it, diabolical.'

I smiled. 'I know, brother.'

He blushed. 'I promised to stand by Maria if she decided to throw over Rushworth and came to live with me.'

'And Edmund gave me every indication he would make me his wife.'

It took all my powers of persuasion; but in the end, Henry did my bidding, as I knew he would. For I had in the meantime contacted Mr Yates and, in return for my discretion, secured a new start in life for Henry and me.

'Thank you, Mary,' Henry said, and kissed me, when I revealed my plan to him. 'I would not mind putting some distance between Maria and me.'

I returned his kiss. 'You will soon forget her in the excitement of our passage to the East Indies.'

And that is how we came to be in Calcutta, the city whose wealth and grandeur puts London to shame. We have changed our names, and we can finally live exactly as we please. We have everything in abundance, palaces, servants, jewels, and lovers. Henry keeps a *zenana* of *bibis*, while I have my pick of Bengal's most dashing and wealthy Englishmen.

And not just Englishmen; I have plenty of European admirers, whom I visit when I take my *budgerow* on the Ganges, up to Chandernagore, the French settlement, and Chinsura, the Dutch trading post. We own properties in Calcutta, Alipur, and Hugli; and each of our houses far surpasses Mansfield Park in ostentation and splendour. Do you have white marble halls exported from Italy, peacock-patterned tiles from Turkey, and crimson silk carpets from Persia? I do, just so you know.

I spend my days at the Western Shop, where I acquire everything that is expensive and exquisite, ivory carved into chairs, damask cloths lined with silver threads, agate jewel boxes decorated with solid diamond clasps. I bathe in attar of roses, drink champagne from golden cups, and eat sesame cakes doused in camel milk. I do everything that pleases and nothing that disgusts me, since I have no one to answer to but myself.

Are you envious, Fanny Price? I hope against hope that you might be, since your Mansfield Park-begot respectability is as nothing to my unimaginable East Indian luxury. But you are not, are you? You, who exist in voluntary simplicity, will never desire the things I value so greatly. Shame on you, Fanny Price! I am writing, not to make you covetous, since that would be useless, but to prick your conscience at last. You could have saved me, but instead you chose to forsake me. How could you be so uncaring towards a woman who wished only to be your friend?

If pity is akin to love, I loved you the moment I set eyes on you. You were so timid and self-effacing, I read in your expression that, like me, you were the niece of a tyrannical uncle, who survived only because she allowed herself to be abused. I imagined Sir Thomas to share the same vicious nature as Admiral Crawford, who had come to my bedroom and forced himself on me, ever since I was a child. It was for this reason that I was kind to you – I wished to help you find a way out of your servility. When you began to assert yourself under my tutelage, I felt proud. I also felt you were beholden to me.

But you were never thankful for my efforts. First impressions made you dislike me and, stubborn as you are – you would call it 'steadfast,' but Fanny Price, inflexibility is as unpleasant a character trait as inconsistency – you refused to change your mind about me. Well, in any case, the tie that I assumed bound us was based on a grave misunderstanding. You were imposed upon, but not by Sir Thomas. It was Mrs Norris who oppressed you, sending you to cut roses in the sun.

Poor Fanny. Gardening in the heat? Sleep in a wintery attic? Was that the extent of your suffering? Yes? Then please do not ask me to feel sorry for you. There are worse fates. Little girls who do not know why they are being punished by their uncles… little boys who hold their ears, so that they do not have to listen to their sisters crying out in pain…

That was the story of my youth, and I had no Edmund. But I had a Henry, and when he reached majority, he took me away from the Admiral, so that I would be safe. But as we lived and traveled together, he found out, to his horror, that he desired me, too. That is why we took refuge at the Grants, and why he courted other women. He tried hard not to emulate his uncle's shameful conduct.

Then, in the midst of his obsession, Henry encountered a vision of goodness, Fanny Price and her brother William, a sibling relationship rendered remarkable by its innocence and purity. *Your* innocence, Fanny Price, *your* purity, so fine, so strong, he hoped it would exorcise his demon. That is why he begged you to save him, but you refused – and made him lose heart forevermore.

When Edmund cast me out, Henry hastened to my side to comfort me, and I was in such dire need of succour, we finally broke that most ancient taboo. Do you know, Fanny Price, that oriental men bed their sisters? Not that I care, it is all the same to me. Family means nothing any longer, only self-indulgence, and I intend never to worry about my passage home.

I am still beautiful, bright, and sparkling. Like a lovely vessel, I drift between Calcutta and Chinsura, waiting for the day when the Ganges will tire of my burden and make me sink to the ground. Only Henry will mourn me then; if he is still alive, that is. There is little chance, since no one survives for long in Calcutta, and he likes his opium, drink, and women rather too well these days. Eight bottles of port, three *bibis*, and two pipes by sunrise: that is his regimen, as if he tried to divert himself into an early grave.

Death and luxury; that is all I think about these days. But once, when I was young, I longed for love and friendship; and I thought I had found them both at Mansfield Park. So what if I also wanted wealth and well-being? So what, if I wanted it *all*…? Must the secret of life be moderation? Do we humans always have to strive for the golden mean? And what about you, Fanny Price, did humility give you everything you wanted? Do you feel you have triumphed over me in the end?

What were the odds? Whom would you have backed, had you been in the audience – outsider Fanny, or the favourite Mary, in the race to win the great prize of Mansfield Park? Now, be honest. Anyone with eyes and ears would surely have put their money on me. Why then, did I lose? Even years later, I still fail to make sense of my final days at Mansfield Park. Why did Edmund not appreciate my counsel? And why did he cease to adore me? Why do I even ask? I know the answer. It was you who made him revile me, who incited him to send me away.

You have blood on your hands, Fanny Price, the blood of my heart, which you pierced when you encouraged Edmund to betray me. Tell me, did it ever occur to you that I could have sued him for breach of promise? Or were you not aware that he had asked me to be his wife? Well that is why I am writing. I'll have you understand that I was sacrificed, *that I sacrificed myself,* so that you could become *Fanny Bertram*. So now you know. You only exist because I paid the price for your happiness, since that is how the world works. For every woman who finds a home where she may live out her days serene and contented, another is sent into exile to appease the fates.

You owe me, in o, so many ways. Now all that remains is for me to ask you to pray for me and to seek my forgiveness. Otherwise, I swear, I will haunt you in your dreams.

Yours in perpetuity,

Mary Crawford

Bibi – English term for an Indian mistress or common-law wife
Budgerow – a large barge or houseboat, rowed by a crew of men
Zenana – a seraglio or house of women

THE TELLTALE SIGNS

Jocelyn Watson

After we arrived home I went straight to bed but had a restless night. I tossed and turned, getting up, walking round the room, getting back into bed, hot even with a light cotton sheet. The whole night I was edgy; couldn't lie still; desperate for someone to speak to. Though I thought about waking Mama, I knew that the person I really wanted to talk to was Rakel. As light seeped through the shutters, I became aware that the day had arrived. When I looked at myself in the mirror my face looked as pale as the Goan women who put on face powder to whiten their skin. Pulling back the shutters I looked out; the muted blue light calmed me and the high-pitched drone of the cicadas distracted me for a few moments. Throwing a shawl over my shoulders, I walked out of my room to find Arkanj wiping the tiles. I smiled and whispered, 'Morning — *diu borrey des*. Come drink chai with me, Arkanj.'

Arkanj hadn't finished but I dragged her to the kitchen. It was already a hive of activity, with a rich aroma of different spices and masalas. Colours flooded the kitchen: fragrant green chopped dhanyia and dark green tongues of spinach. Large red clay pots were filled with peeled garlic and crushed ginger. Stainless steel containers were filled with fresh coconut milk, jar after jar of red, green, yellow, brown seeds and spices that Candida was ready to mix together as part of her contribution to the wedding festivities. I poured out milky, sweet, spicy chai from the steaming handi into four stainless steel cups. Candida wanted me to taste some of her dishes but I couldn't; I was feeling sicker and sicker. Arkanj, Bibiana and Candida dismissed it all as wedding nerves.

'Everybody happy today.' Arkanj winked and her gold front tooth glinted as she smiled.

I sat with them and quietly sipped my chai. But they were busy and so I soon manoeuvred my way around the baskets, bamboo containers, clay pots and jute sacks of rice and pulses and slipped out of the kitchen. I stared at the hand-painted murals on the wall, of grey fluffy-tailed cats, large black-faced long-limbed monkeys, strident tigers and charismatic, gentle deer. This was the last time I would share chai with these familiar creatures and with Arkanj, Bibiana and Candida.

Soon the sound of stirring emerged from the otherwise silent rooms of the house. Bibiana was being called from every room. I had my bucket bath, and with each jug of water that I poured over my body, I tried to understand why I was in such a state. I threw on my faded purple cotton shalwar kameez and went into Mama and Papa's room. Mama asked me to help her find her noratin gold necklace set so I rifled through her suitcase and found the red pouch and took out the nine-gemmed gold set. I placed the necklace, the ring, the dangling triangular earrings, adorned with tiny rubies and sapphires and the other precious noratin stones, on the dressing table.

'Your Papa bought these for me in Bombay after we were married, just before he brought me to England.'

I smiled and left Mama as she was beginning to wrap her orange and yellow silk embroidered sari around her petticoat, and returned to my own room. It was a different house. The peace and quiet had transformed into bustle and activity: people eating breakfast, the men having cigarettes, children running through the rooms, Charlotte and Jane getting their families clothed and fed, strangers walking through the house and garden, switching on fairy lights, carrying cutlery, crockery, plants, lanterns, boxes and ginny bags. By ten o'clock the house was in complete pandemonium. I was still standing, leaning against the wall in my bedroom.

When I eventually opened my door the chaos had subsided; things seemed to be where they were supposed to be, and the men were all spruced up in their English linen suits. They stared at me as I peeked out, still wearing my faded purple shalwar kameez. I hastily shut the door and leant back against it, and just as I was trying to gather myself, there was a knock.

'Who is it?' I asked nervously.

'It's Rakel.'

I opened the door. She was dressed in a simple lavender shalwar kameez with a fine silver embroidered border and a matching dupatta. I stared at her; the silver added light to her eyes and a glow to her cheeks. Her drooping silver pearl earrings and the fine line of black kohl around her eyes made them stand out more dramatically than ever. I stared at her, thinking I had never seen her look so stunning. 'Wow. Lovely. Your eyes. You do, you look dazzling.'

'Enough already. You're the wedding girl and you need to get a move on. Everybody is dressed and you're still wearing—'

'I...'

'Are you going to do that English thing; bride always arriving late and all...?'

'Rakel...'

'Hurry now, put these on.' She picked up the beige silk churidahs.

'Rakel, I can't.'

'Anne, I never thought of you as a drama queen!'

I took hold of her hands and clasped them tightly in mine.

'*Arrey*, careful, you'll ruin Arkanj's ironing and she'll have to do it all over again.'

'Rakel, Rakel, where are you? Come now.' Auntie Flavia was calling.

Rakel looked at me and shrugged her shoulders as though to say she would rather stay but had better go. I watched her leave the room and heard her directing those new to the house: commenting and congratulating everyone on how they looked, organising people for the convoys of cars that were waiting outside.

After she had left I was alone in the room. Auntie Flavia and Jacinta and Mama walked in and, seeing me in my half-dressed state, started to busy themselves dressing me. Everyone's eyes were focussed on me, and I had nowhere and no one to look to for respite.

By the time Rakel came back into the room I was dressed. Mama had put make-up on my face and had done my hair, and Auntie Flavia and Jacinta were fussing over the fall of the dupatta. A posse of Ambassador cars had been commandeered for the day.

I stepped out of the car at St. Cajetan's Church to Papa's reassuring arms.

'Anne you look lovely,' said Auntie Elant.

'*Shabash*,' remarked Mr Kamat, looking distinguished in his pristine white dhoti, his long black coat and cap.

'My dear, you look absolutely wonderful,' Mrs Pinto smiled.

Before I could say anything Papa had begun to escort me towards Father Ignatius standing at the entrance of St. Cajetan. The church was filled with the aroma of incense and burning candles. The procession was led by altar boys in their red and white habits followed by priests from North Goa adorned in elaborate brocaded vestments. The older priests had known Mama's family for decades.

When I looked across the pews it was to a congregation adorned in colour, a harvest of flowers and decorations with a multitude of smiling faces. My stomach began to heave.

Light poured through the stained glass windows onto the brass statutes of Christ and the Virgin Mary and onto the women in their yellow and green and purple saris and dresses, and the men in sherwanis and suits, and onto the dusty perfumed haze from the candles and incense that enveloped the church.

Robeiro stood at the altar waiting for me. I looked at him as he smiled at me; a loving smile; a warm glowing smile; a smile from a handsome, generous human being.

'Papa, take me out of here. Papa, please. Papa, please.' Though I didn't shout Papa could hear the frenzy in my voice.

He stopped. The organ and the church choir continued though we remained stationary. Robeiro's smile turned to a confused gaze when we didn't proceed. His bright eyes looked across at me in bewilderment.

'Papa, please. Please take me out.'

Papa turned me around. Though it was barely audible I could hear everyone gasp and whisper. The singing and playing continued as Papa and I walked out of the church. Within minutes there was the swish of saris following behind. We stood in the courtyard, Papa, Mama, Charlotte and Jane, Auntie Flavia and Jacinta. Rakel stood in the doorway.

'I can't go through with this.'

Papa held me in his arms as I cried.

They all tried to talk to me, to calm me, to reassure me that how I felt was natural and that all brides experienced similar anxiety. Papa held onto me tightly and finally when he sensed that, for whatever reasons, I genuinely couldn't go through with it all, he indicated to the others that they should desist.

Mama was distraught. 'What are we going to do?'

Jacinta took Mama's hand. 'I'll go in and tell Father Ignatius.'

Papa held me gently in his arms as I continued crying, and eventually he wrapped his arm around my shoulders and escorted me down the hill where we got into one of the waiting cars. He told the driver to drive north.

We took the ferry across the Chapora River and Papa instructed the driver to keep driving. Then, on the top of one of the smaller hills, he spotted a tiny restaurant, and told the driver to take us there. He ordered himself a whisky. I shook my head and he ordered me a juice, and we sat there looking out onto the sea. He didn't speak and neither did I. We sat in silence looking out ahead: occasionally a flicker of dark black dots rose up on the surface of the water: boats and yachts and Goan fishing vessels sailing past.

Papa patted my hand but didn't seek to find words because there were none. We stayed till the sun set and the light was replaced by a blackened sky. After what must have been several hours, the driver drove us back to the house. I looked around, reminding myself that only a short time before I hadn't quite appreciated what I was going through.

I learnt that everyone had remained sitting in church. The choir and the organist finally stopped singing and playing. Jacinta had walked up to Father Ignatius and whispered in his ear and he had led Robeiro into the sacristy. The congregation had sat patiently waiting until Father Ignatius announced that there would be no wedding. All the de Sousas had then left.

As I stared out at the beautiful mirrored marquee still up in the garden, I felt a soft hand on my arm.

'Are you all right?' Rakel stared into my face looking concerned.

'Yes… No,' I said. I didn't know where to look or what to say. 'I feel so bad.'

'Everyone who came has left. Charlotte and Jane have been very supportive: talking to people and calming your mother.'

'What can I say? I'm so grateful they were here.'

'Your Auntie and Jacinta, too, were very reassuring. The priests and nuns were escorted to their seats by your mother and the family. Of course the de Sousas left church straightaway. Auntie Flavia and Jacinta and the other relatives looked after the priests and nuns.'

Candida's two tiered white wedding cake sat untouched on the centre table. I knew that Candida had worked on it each morning for the past week.

'What are you going to do?'

'I don't know.'

'Anne,' Mama called and I left Rakel and walked over to her. She opened her arms and clutched hold of me as we both cried.

'Are you all right, sweetie?'

'Mama I feel so bad.'

Mama lifted her shoulders and held out her hands.

'I was sure and then it all came unstuck.'

'Why, darling, why?'

'Oh, Mama, it was when I was in the church I realised I couldn't go through with it.'

'I'm so sad for you.'

'It wasn't fair to Robeiro.'

Mama stroked my hair as I cried. 'Your Auntie and Jacinta have arranged for the rest of the food to be distributed.'

'All the money, the preparation...'

'Your Papa and I will pay for all the expenses incurred by Vincent and Esther de Sousa and their family; so don't worry about that for now. But darling you must go and speak to Robeiro and tell him.'

In the days that followed, it was decided that I would return to the UK with Mama and Papa. All the excursions that had been arranged for the cousins, aunties and uncles were cancelled, and everyone was left to decide whether they wanted to stay or go. I went and apologised to Mr and Mrs de Sousa. They were cold and distant.

Robeiro was forgiving and gracious and hurt. There wasn't a great deal I could say. My desperate, pathetic attempts to explain that initially I had thought I was panicking over nothing, and had listened gratefully as everyone kept telling me it was nerves, didn't help him. I kept repeating that he deserved someone who would always be in love with him. He looked bereft. He stared at me with his forlorn gaze. He couldn't understand and I couldn't explain.

Rakel was the last person to whom I said farewell.

'I'm sorry I made such a mess of things.'

'You could have just gone through with it and then lived to regret it.'

'I hate myself.'

'Anne, why don't you stay? Give yourself some time.'

'I can't, Rakel. I can't bear the thought of seeing Robeiro after all that I've done. I can't face them all, though I shall miss you terribly.'

'Maybe we'll see each other when you come to Goa again.'

'I don't know when that'll be.'

When the drivers came to take us to the airport I cried, as did Auntie Flavia and Joy, Arkanj, Bibiana and Candida. Auntie Flavia gave me a warm hug saying, 'Remember, Anne, you never know what lies ahead.'

I don't think I've ever been on such a lonely plane journey. I began to understand that I had almost become trapped in a relationship that, once the honeymoon period was over, would have been soul-destroying and unhappy, and not just for me, but for Robeiro as well. It had been obvious to Rakel, not to me, until now. I could never have been the acquiescent wife that Robeiro, despite his claims to the contrary, wanted and needed. However much he admired what he saw, he would have found it hard to reconcile the differences when they arose. I couldn't conform to what was expected of me when I knew it would eventually cause a great deal of unhappiness. I resigned myself to an empty life though Auntie Flavia's words echoed in my mind.

'You're an independent woman, Anne. I honestly don't think you could have acquiesced to being a dutiful wife.'

'You're right. But so bizarre that it required me leaving England, coming to Goa and almost marrying Robeiro before I truly understood myself.'

MY NAME IS KATHERINE BURROWS

Mary Fitzpatrick

My name is Katherine Burrows and I was born eighty-five years ago, right here in this pretty, couthy wee town. In summer, the sun shines on the tourists as well as on the swallows jinking and diving all along the main street, but in autumn a cauld wind begins to skitter leaves across cobbles and up closes; with winter the watercolour houses – ivy green, peacock blue, cyclamen pink – run and bleed in the rain. Oh, aye, a pretty wee town, a couthy wee town, but lonely when ye get tae eighty-five and naebody wants ye…

As ye can see I'm feelin sorry for myself today. Why? Because when I went intae the kitchen this morn and looked at the calendar I noticed that it's the fourth of April and a wee voice in my dumbfoonered brain said, 'April fourth? Noo why is that date special?' And then I remembered, it's Edward's birthday. And, oh, I so wanted tae see him, right that minute, I wanted him to walk intae the kitchen and put his long arms around me saying, 'Auntie Kate, long time no see…'

But, och, that made me feel auld. But then, I *am* auld. My joints are sore and stiff, so stiff that often in the morn I have to slide down the stairs on my backside. I can't straighten my hands – they're like ancient roots, full of boles and knots. For a long time my eyes were clouded and milky with cataracts, that is until last year when I had a wee op and – bingo! – I can see again, everything so bright and sharp I almost wished I could go back to that soft haziness of before. It's nearly too much, this clarity of vision.

I have to admit that my memory is also a bit mixter-maxter, that's to say, some days are better than others, and there are some things it's a blessing to forget. Yet, this morning, when I thought of Edward came this lovely memory of him standing in the garden, a wee boy in short trousers blowing bubbles towards my Ann as she danced and clapped and tried to catch the rainbows which hovered over her head. How patient he was with her, how gentle. How I loved that boy, he was like my own.

My sister, his mother, would laugh and say, 'Kate, yer smothering the boy!' every time I clasped him to me. But he never tried to break away, he just allowed me the pleasure of hugging his sturdy, strong body to mine, then I'd let him go and we'd carry the picnic out to eat below the big apple tree: cheese and oatcakes and apples and buttered scones and, to drink, tea in the big tartan flask.

When we watched them play, Edward and Ann, I'd often say, 'They're a braw pair, aren't they?' I had this idea, you see, that one day he and my girl might marry, they would have bairns: dark, clear eyed lads like Edward and shy, blue eyed lassies like Ann. They'd visit every Sunday and...

But my sister would shake her head, looking at me out of the corner of her eye in that queer, sly way she had, saying, 'Oh, Kate, don't talk nonsense. They're *cousins*, it wouldnae be right for them to marry.'

And I'd just nod as if I agreed but inside me I was saying, 'We'll see, we'll see.'

In the year Edward turned ten my sister began to complain of pains in her chest and throat. At my suggestion she took to drinking a cordial distilled from the mayflowers; by the time she went to see Doctor Baxter her already skinny body was ravaged and, by Hallowe'en, she was gone. After she died Edward came to live with us, me and Ann and his Uncle Tam, God rest his soul. His faither agreed to this because he was away on the boats and couldn't look after the boy; he was a waster, a drinker, but at least he knew that the boy was better off with us.

How we loved the sound of a boy in the house, clattering up the stairs, bringing in aw sorts from the hedgerows and lochans then sitting in the parlour wae Ann, helping her wae her homework, two heads bent ower their books, one dark, one blonde. I'd watch them from the kitchen and my heart would near burst wae happiness.

My Ann's away in Edinburgh noo, running a veggie café, of aw things. I hardly ever see her but she does phone at weekends, she's no a bad lass. She's livin wae a woman called Marta, I met her the once, nice enough woman but I didn't know whit tae make of her clothes, awfy mannish they were. Her and Ann sat in the front room eating cherry cake and drinking tea and looking right uncomfortable.

When I asked Ann if she ever heard from Edward she just rolled

78

her eyes and said, 'Mother, I'd say Edward and *Lizzie* are rather busy running their law practice in Australia.'

'Don't mention that one's name in my house.'

'You could always Skype,' says Marta, hanging onto my best Prince Albert cup and saucer, a bit like a Clydesdale cradling a thimble.

'Whit?' I said.

'*Skype*, Mum.' Ann sighed and made that face, the one that makes her mouth look like a cat's bum. 'I explained it to you before, it's on the internet…'

And on and on she went, internet this, connections that, and I wanted to say, 'I don't want to see Edward's face on ony bloody screen, I want him *here*, sitting next tae me on the auld horsehair sofa, the way he used to do, telling me stories aboot the world outside.'

So as she talked and talked I just thocht aboot the good auld times, walking on the beach at Southerness or up at the loch ootside Kirkcudbright, him skimming stones and Ann paddling, then walking through the woods, away hame for supper, all of us happy, all of us *together*.

We wanted Edward tae take ower the running of the shop after his Uncle Tam passed away but, naw, the dominie had other ideas, the boy was bright, he should be at the uni, not stuck behind the counter of a hardware store. So, at seventeen off he went to Glasgow, seeing him go nearly broke my heart and I thought Ann would take it fair bad as well but she just shrugged and said, 'He's only away to Glasgow, for God's sake, not Mars.' Oh, she's an awfy queer one when she's got a mind tae be.

But he soon settled in, everything going swimmingly, until one day in his second year he comes home wae this big galloot called Billy Bingham, one of thae posh hippy types, aw teeth and hair. He was too much of a gadfly and he started taking Edward tae pubs and clubs and dances where, sure enough, he met all kinds of wee madams, if ye pardon my language. And it was at one of those dances that he met *her*, that Lizzie one. Turned out that Billy Bingham fancied her big sister Janey and he wanted them all to go out as a foursome. Edward told me this one weekend, home wae all his dirty laundry, the wee devil. He was sitting at our kitchen table wolfing into his favourite, scotch broth wae homemade bannocks. 'Och, Auntie Kate,' he said, 'I do miss yer cooking...'

He seemed reluctant to tell me about her, this Lizzie, but I winkled it out of him, how he wasn't sure at first, she was a bit too full of herself, a bit of a *feminist*, but then when he glanced up from his food I saw it, the light in his beautiful eyes and that look, somewhere between puzzlement and wonder, the sure sign of love.

I put my hand to my mouth, I had to, to still the trembling there. I took a wee sip of tea and said in a voice as steady as I could make it, 'But, Edward, son, I always thocht that you and Ann...' I stopped, not knowing how to go on.

He frowned and said, 'Ann? Me and Ann? But Auntie Kate don't you realise...' He stopped and gently put his hand over mine and I couldnae stop the tears from spilling down my face.

When she came to visit she was wearing a dress made of cheap striped cotton that you could spit peas through and a funny wee straw hat wae yellow flowers, it was March and she was shivering so much she nearly shook them aff the brim. She'd a funny accent tae, a mixture of what sounded like English and French and I wondered what kind of family did she come from; when she told me she had four sisters I wondered if they were maybe Papists, wae a family that size. A wee, young scrape of a thing that you could've put in yer pocket, but when I looked intae her face I knew that I was beaten, with her firm mouth and knowing eyes and that fine, glistening strawberry gold hair.

I asked her to help me make the tea in the kitchen. When we were alone I said, 'Well, do you intend to marry my Edward?'

She stood swirling the hot water in the teapot and looked at me mockingly. '*Your* Edward?' she said and I swear I would have slapped her wee face if Edward and Ann hadn't been sitting next door. Then she continued, coolly, with a shrug of her narrow shoulders, 'I haven't committed myself to anything, I regard marriage as somewhat patriarchal but...if we make the leap you'll be the first to know, *Auntie*

Kate.' And with that she emptied the pot down the sink and marched out of the kitchen.

During the day I mostly sit at the window, watching the bairns in the school opposite playing in the yard, the seagulls rooting through the chip papers, the shadows of the sycamores dancing in the watery glass. From here I can also see the town stocks still on their original site, kept, I suppose, as a reminder to all the fate of those who break the rules. Oh, aye, it's what they call a busy window.

A lovely Polish lass called Patrizia comes into help me, making my porridge in the morn, heating up my soup at night. Tonight she came in to give me a bath and, boy, it was quite a palaver. Where did the days go when I jooked in and oot of the tin bath sitting in front of the fire? Gone, long gone. Afterwards, lying on the bed wrapped up in the nice big fluffy dressing gown Ann gave me at Christmas, I was just like a big baby, with Patrizia gently brushing the few remaining hairs on my auld pink scalp. I used to mind going bald but not anymore – what's the use of vanity at my age? But, as I say, I felt like a child in swaddling clothes till a thought occurred, 'No, Kate, you're nearer the grave than the cradle now.'

I asked Patrizia to fetch me the photograph album and I leafed through it slowly, the pictures of me and Tam, Edward and Ann. But I was searching for the ones of Edward and Lizzie's wedding, and there they were, him so handsome in his cream linen suit, dark curly hair tousled in the spring breeze, her looking daft in a tartan dress and – heaven save us – red lace up boots, Doc Martens they're called, or so Ann told me.

I squinted at them and shook my head. I've only got the photos, you see, I didn't go to the wedding, even though Edward begged me and Lizzie sent me a letter, asking me to come as a special favour to him. But, no, I was stubborn, I let Ann go in my stead. Turned out I was right, turned out the Bennets are a funny bunch, faither one of those head in the clouds, academic fellas, mother a screechy auld midden who got fair drunk on the sherry. One of the sisters kept on grabbing the microphone and singing when everyone else wanted her

81

to shut up and sit down; eventually her faither had to go up and take the microphone away, just to quieten her.

As I looked at the photos I began to doze and before ye know it I was away, up, up in the corner of the room, floating, looking down at myself and I saw that I wasn't lying in my bed but in my coffin, with Patrizia getting me ready for the grave. It gave me a right turn, that did, I shouted for Patrizia to come and she did, tucking me in with a nice wee cuppa.

I reached once again for the photo album and turned to another picture, right at the back of the collection, the one of Edward and Lizzie and their two braw bairns, Edward and – would you credit it? – Katherine, all looking so fine and handsome, sitting under a stripy brolly on the beach, somewhere in Australia. I closed the album and put it to one side, the tea sitting on the bedside table growing scummy and cold as I lay staring at the big pink peony roses on the wallpaper. It's coming, I know, the thing that I've tried not to think about all the time I've lived alone in this house. But it's coming, maybe not tonight, but sometime soon, it can't be avoided, and as I turned to switch off the light a question entered my head, like a ghost whispering in my ear: 'Oh, Edward, Edward, my boy – what have I done?'

MARY'S SILVER KNIFE

Janet Lee

The ghost of Mary looked out of the window and saw her brother alight from the carriage. She had of course heard the talk of the past few days, since the letter arrived, and she knew William was coming home. That he was bringing Fanny sent a shiver of excitement through Mary. Fanny had long since gone to the Bertrams and had not visited Portsmouth since she first left.

Mary had not seen Fanny since her own death. She knew she must find a way to make Fanny hear her.

The Price house in Portsmouth was always full of noise, which made it hard for a ghost to be heard. The smallness of the house, the thinness of its walls and the many inhabitants, ensured a lot of competition for sound.

Although she had died so young, Mary already knew of ghost stories in which women in white moaned and floated, and headless men rattled chains. Such noise would not be heard above the din of the Price household, with the constant bustle, stomping on floors, slamming of doors and the boys forever tumbling up and down the stairs.

And even though the succession of maids were slovenly, leaving plenty of dust for messages, when Mary tried to write in the dirt, it was quickly covered with a new layer, or disturbed by the children and their rough play.

It was hard to be a ghost in the Price household.

Betsey was still able to hear her, but for how long, Mary couldn't be sure. Betsey was young and still taken with the murmurings of a ghost. She did not yet know that such things were of another world, and so assumed Mary was one of her imaginary play friends. Mary often spoke to Betsey, both to have a friend and hear her chatter, they were after all, of a similar age, but also out of the sheer boredom of being trapped in such a house. Mary would play quietly with Betsey, and try to stop her from being naughty or tantruming, not always with success.

Her little brothers, although also young, were not easy for Mary to speak with. They were too noisy to hear the whispers of a ghost and too rough to notice her passing.

Her sister Susan had been able to hear her, and might yet again, but she too was trapped in this house and worn down and fractious with its cares.

Her parents were a lost cause. No, it would have to be Fanny. Fanny was her only hope of escape.

The din in the hallway told Mary that Fanny had settled into the parlour. Mary waited until William came upstairs to dress, then she smoothed her hair and drifted down the stairs to see her sister.

When Mary entered the parlour, her father and Fanny were seated in opposite corners of the small room. They were not speaking, and their manner was not one of comfortable silence. He was reading the paper and Fanny had shrunk back into her seat in her corner, seemingly unoccupied, her hands held still in her lap. There was only one candle and it was being used by their father to read his paper.

In the semi-darkness of the room, Mary was able to observe her sister, without being noticed, because no one in the house seemed to see her save Betsey, and she was in the other room. But Mary had hoped Fanny might see her, or see her shadow, flicked upon the wall by candlelight.

She stood, somewhat shyly and smiled, 'Hello, Fanny.'

Fanny looked up and turned her head to glance around the room as though searching for something and, for a moment, Mary's heart lurched, hoping her sister had felt her presence.

'Fanny! Fanny!' Mary cried, and stepped forward.

'Devil take those young dogs!' called their father. 'How they are singing out.'

Fanny looked up toward the hallway door, in the direction of the noisy brothers. Mary then realised Fanny had been lost in her own thoughts, listening to the noise of the house. She had not seen or heard Mary at all.

Despondent, Mary stopped and stared at her sister. Fanny was a grown woman now. Of course, thought Mary, she has aged and I have not, I have just grown solemn.

Fanny sat with a sweet, genteel manner and looked quite out of place in the Prices' small parlour. She was no longer a part of the rabble of this house and Mary could see she felt it keenly. She was not much changed, just an older version of the sweet simple girl Mary could picture cuddling her as a child, or nursing Tom as a baby.

The boys burst into the gloom of the parlour and proceeded to sit and poke and tease each other. A bustle at the door presented the start of tea and their mother and sisters followed. Mary realised the quiet moment to speak with Fanny was gone. Instead, she watched as Fanny tried to listen attentively while her mother warbled on about the servants.

But she must keep trying, so Mary crept up beside Fanny.

With Fanny sitting, Mary was able to stand on her toes and place her arm about her and lay her head upon Fanny's shoulder.

'Did you weep for me, Fanny, when you heard I had died, did you weep?' she whispered.

Fanny didn't seem to notice Mary. In a moment Fanny stood from her chair as William came into the room, resplendent in his Lieutenant's uniform, tears springing to her eyes at the sight.

Mary tried again, aware an emotional time provided an opportunity for a ghost.

'Talk of me, dear sister, remember me,' Mary pleaded.

Fanny did not move, although Mary continued to whisper.

'I am Mary, think of me, remember me.'

Fanny sat back in her place and wiped her eyes, moved only by the sight of William in his splendid uniform.

Mary knew Fanny could neither hear nor see her. She would need to think of some other way. Perhaps Fanny would hear her through Betsey.

Betsey was sitting on a low stool across from Fanny, and she could see Mary clearly. She was watching Mary hug and plead with their sister.

So Mary went to Betsey and sat beside her, whispering in her ear, 'Touch your curls, my dear Betsey, twist them between your fingers like this.'

Betsey did this and became the picture of a sweet angelic child.

Mary saw Fanny look over and felt a thrill of recognition in Fanny's face.

Fanny was silent as she looked at Betsey. The child was playing with her curls in the same gentle way, twirling them between finger and thumb just as Mary had done. Fanny even imagined she saw a faint glow about the child.

Mary could sense Fanny remembering.

'Yes, yes,' she urged.

'The same little curls. The same pretty ways,' Fanny murmured to herself.

Mary sprang back to Fanny and kissed her gently on the cheek, 'Yes, sister, think of me, say my name, say my name!'

Fanny continued to look at Betsey, 'the same little curls', she said again.

Mary could sense Fanny's hesitation, but she knew she must act before the moment was gone. She went back to Betsey and, twirling her curls, whispered, 'the knife, Betsey, get my knife, you know you want to show Fanny my knife don't you?'

Betsy looked up at Mary, to others it would have appeared the happy thought of a child, smiling at some remembrance.

Mary nodded a reassurance.

'Yes, Betsey, good girl, the knife.'

Betsey slid her hand into the pocket of her pinny; Mary knew she had hidden the knife there when she found the shirt sleeve for her mother. It had been in the kitchen drawer.

'Show Fanny the knife, Betsey, let Fanny see it first, just Fanny,' Mary urged.

Betsey held the knife, angling it to catch Fanny's eye, but at the same time shielding it from Susan.

Fanny saw it.

'What have you got there, my love?' Fanny said. 'Come and show it to me.'

As Mary had hoped, Susan, jumped up claiming the knife as hers, as indeed it was. Betsey ran to their mother's side.

'It is very hard that I am not to have my *own* knife,' Susan said.

'Mary left it to me on her deathbed, and I ought to be allowed to keep it, but Mamma is always letting Betsey take it and she will spoil it.'

'Now, Susan,' Mrs Price said, 'now how can you be so cross? You are always quarrelling about that knife. I wish you would not be so quarrelsome. Poor little Betsey; how cross Susan is to you! But you should not have taken it out, my dear, when I sent you to the drawer. I must hide it another time. Poor little Mary thought it would be such a bone of contention when she gave it to me to keep, only two hours before she died. Poor little soul! She could but just speak to be heard, and she said so prettily, "Let Susan have my knife, Mamma, when I am dead and buried." Poor little dear! She was so fond of it, Fanny, that she would have it lay by her in bed, all through her illness. It was the gift of her good godmother, old Mrs Admiral Maxwell, only six weeks before she was taken for death. Poor sweet little creature.'

Fanny bowed her head in remembrance of Mary.

Mary smiled.

Finally her name had been said and she knew Fanny thought of her. Now… to make her do what she wanted.

In the weeks which followed, Mary tried to get Fanny to hear her. Now her name had been mentioned it may be easier for her sister. Mary whispered in Fanny's ear while she slept, the only time there would be any peace in this house of noise, disorder and impropriety. She clung to Fanny in the parlour, while Fanny sewed for Sam. Fanny seemed not to hear her. Yet Mary kept trying, whispering, begging, and pleading into Fanny's ears whenever Fanny was still. But Mary was not aware if Fanny thought of her little sister again. Until the day Fanny chose to buy Betsey her own knife.

Mary saw Fanny leave, but she herself was bound to the house and unable to follow, and so she did not know what errand Fanny was upon. It was only when Fanny returned that Mary became aware of the purchase she had made.

A new silver knife was given to Betsey, who declared it with every advantage over the silver knife of Susan's. Susan was established to have full possession of her own knife. She was relieved by this and thereafter, kept it in the room she shared with Fanny, next to her bed, just as Mary had done.

Mary was beside herself with excitement.

She knew Fanny could hear her whispers.

Because Fanny had done just what Mary had asked her.

Now to get her to do the next thing for Mary.

With the arrival of Mr Crawford, Mary lost her opportunities to speak with Fanny. Her sister seemed agitated and preoccupied and Mary could not be sure if Fanny thought of her at all.

As the weeks of Fanny's visit ran past, Mary saw letters arriving for her, and how concerned she was as she pondered the contents. Mary knew all was not well yet she continued to whisper into Fanny and Susan's ears while they slept, hoping they would hear her. Mary was urging Fanny to take Susan into Northamptonshire and encouraging Susan to long for the event to happen.

As with all who die, Mary had been bound to something after her own death. Not her grave, surely, not that sad little plot at the rear of the churchyard, unmarked and unkempt, flowered only by the wild grasses and visited by no one.

Not to the house in Portsmouth, shut in forever to the noise and bustle and the 'evils of home', with no sketch in remembrance of Mary to be taken out and gently pondered. Her own clothes had long been re-made and re-used. Though she was trapped in its walls for now, there was nothing of Mary in this house. No, it would be to her silver knife that she would cling. It would be that which would be her talisman and remembrance. Her one reminder to the world that she had existed. Given with love by her godmother, cherished by Mary as she lay dying, and bequeathed with love to her own sister.

Mary's silver knife would travel with her sisters as they journeyed into Northamptonshire. That knife would become Mary's relic.

And so it was, on the day of their departure for the Bertrams,

90

wrapped in a tiny piece of linen and tucked neatly beside Susan's spare pelisse, Mary's silver knife travelled with Fanny and Susan into Northamptonshire.

And with it went the ghost of Mary Price herself.

---

[1] Jane Austen *Mansfield Park*, chapter 38.

THE AUSTEN FACTOR

Marian Ford

My aunt Philips thinks I'm heading for a fall. She bristles with outrage.

'It didn't surprise me that your younger sisters went off the rails but I thought you had more sense. Mind you…you always were greedy for attention. I blame your—'

I interrupt her. I won't have a bad word spoken about my mother and father unless it's by me. I'm more than happy to complain that it felt as though I had two absentee parents, but as soon as someone else contributes scorn of their own I become strangely protective.

'This could be my way out,' I tell her. 'I thought you'd be pleased.'

She just grunts and starts filling the kettle to make yet another cup of tea. I'm hoping she'll drop the subject but that's not her way.

'Which one are you then?'

'I beg your pardon?'

'You know. The good, the bad or the really bad?'

'I'm still not with you.'

'No one would watch the thing if they just kept the good ones in. They throw out the ones that are only slightly bad – they're boring. But they keep in the ones that are really bad because they make great viewing. What is it they call it – car accident TV?'

'Car crash TV. And no, I don't know which one I am.'

My first is in music but not in song

It's only a mile or so to my house but the sky is a glowering grey and I've never been partial to walking, so I settle down to wait at the bus stop. While I sit there, I worry away at her words. It has taken me the best part of thirty years even to think of running away from home. Maybe Aunt Philips is right, and I've clung on this long hoping to get noticed.

My father complains constantly that I have outstayed my welcome.

'Four down, one to go,' he said, rubbing his hands, when my sister Catherine moved out, and he loves to repeat the refrain, slipping it into the conversation as a taunt whenever I say anything that he considers foolish. But I know it's just his dry sense of humour and that he would hate to see me go, if only because then there would be no one to act as a buffer and spare him from having to listen to his wife.

My mother used to have two interests in life – matchmaking and gossiping about matchmaking. She still congratulates herself on the success she had with my sisters but thankfully has now moved on to thoughts and talk of grandchildren. She has given me up as a lost cause, what with my blunt features and gauche manner. It's a relief, in many ways, to be alone with my books and music, rather than have to attend another of those dispiriting speed dating events at Lucas Lodge Hotel. I know when someone meets me for the first time they are invariably disappointed. My sisters' reputation precedes me, and people are caught off guard at how little I resemble them. I can see the confusion in their eyes, the struggle to bite back questions. I feel like getting a t-shirt printed reading 'No I'm not adopted!' or 'Can't handle the plain truth?'

Maybe she kept hoping to have a boy. All I know is that my mother never had much time for hands-on parenting, was too busy tending to her nerves. By the time my younger sisters came along she was worn out and they were left to grow feral. Our eldest sisters did their best to raise us in her stead. They spun their castoff cotton dresses into gossamer gowns; told us tales of wise girls outsmarting witches, gems that turned to dust, hailstones that changed to pearls. They fashioned toys out of tissue paper and tin cans; invented new rules for old games.

It started with Lydia bawling as we played, taking loud militant sobs, insisting that she be allowed to slither up snakes, lower our counters down ladders.

'Why not just let her?' Jane suggested and Liz approved.

'Well perhaps it wouldn't hurt; there are a lot of social climbing snakes out there in the real world I guess.'

I staged a protest of my own, refused to throw the dice – kept turning it over in my hand, seeing myself in the number five, the lone central dot orbited by four others; seeing my parents on its opposite side, forever distant from us all.

My second is in piano but not in score

Little wonder that Aunt Philips is surprised. I surprised myself by filling out the online application and then by actually going through with it and turning up for the auditions. My sisters used beauty as their key to freedom. I have had to fall back on other gifts. For a long time I pinned my hopes on fleeing to university. My father went to extraordinary lengths to find the money to put his two eldest girls though college: remortgaged the house to finance Jane's medical training; borrowed from his cousin, Bill Collins, to pay for Liz's legal studies. But when it came to the rest of us, he had nowhere left to turn, could unearth no spare funds to supplement a student loan. So I turned to music, hoping it would be my way out. In the event, the first audition seemed more like a test of patience than of musical ability. There must have been thousands of us, packed into the O2 parking lot. Waiting and waiting. Hour after hour. A slow war of attrition. No let-up apart from the sound of muttered protests and, every so often, someone pushing their way past, heading homeward, having had enough. I shut my eyes, feeling the searing sunshine on my face, smelling cloying perfume and sour sweat. Started wondering if I was caught up in a musical version of the dance marathons of the Great Depression. Those without stamina destined to drop out. The last one standing wins. It must have been twelve hours before I was ushered into the vast arena, guided towards one of hundreds of small booths. I couldn't see into the other cubicles, couldn't hear above the noise of competing voices drowning one another out. I performed my songs in front of two people from the production crew, one filming, the other hardly looking at me, so intent was he on tapping at his laptop. I felt sure they'd send me packing but instead they got me to come back and sing again to other members of the team.

I thought that would be it; never expected them to ring; kept dreading the arrival of the post, anticipating the curt rejection note. Even when my father passed me the phone, whispering that De Bourgh Productions were on the line, I thought it must be a hoax call. Since then I have been telling everyone I know, hoping that if I say it enough times I will believe it too.

'I've got through to the next round. They want me to audition for the judges in a week or so.'

I do my best to stay grounded and not let my mind leap ahead to how my life could change. I distract myself by fretting about Christmas. It takes months of mediation to get us all round one table and family fault lines are cruelly exposed. The seating plan alone requires intricate algorithms: my mother is wary of being placed next to Liz's husband, Fitz, and he refuses to sit next to Lydia's husband, George, and so on... Then we have to negotiate our way past the traditional mismatch between gifts. I opt for handmade offerings: make chocolates and embroider cards. Jane is far too generous, treats us to so many exquisite keepsakes, while Lydia spends little money and even less thought on everyone.

I've taken to busking two or three extra afternoons a week. I don't do it for the money – donations are thin on the ground, but I put that down to the recession. No, I do it to share my love of music and bring a bit of much needed culture to Meryton high-street. My favourite spot is next to the covered walkway, outside the Assembly shopping mall. I like to vary the instruments I take along as accompaniment – my pokerwork accordion swathed in black and gold swirls, my willow flute or my descant recorder. People seem to be in such a rush these days and often just scurry past, avoiding eye contact. My voice doesn't carry as well as I'd like, so I wish they'd linger a while to soak up all the subtlety I'm trying to convey. My sister-in-law, Caroline, certainly doesn't seem to appreciate my efforts. Just before Easter, I was in the middle of a performance, building up to a particularly intricate coloratura, when she walked past, laden with bags from Drapers Department store. Caroline didn't even acknowledge me, just stood there for a moment staring, her cheeks flushed fire red, before walking briskly away. I don't think she could have been more embarrassed if I'd been stood in front of Poundland handing out copies of *The Big Issue*.

I've been trying to practise as much as possible. I cry off from work, neglecting my part-time voluntary job at the local National Trust property. Catherine and Lydia have never understood why I would want to be a room attendant there anyway, surrounded by 'the reek of old books and furniture.' You'd think I was working in an abattoir, not Netherfield Park, the way they grimace at the thought.

My third is in perfect but not in pitch

The house dwarfs us now and there is a melancholy to the empty rooms. My mother complains that we should downsize, forces my father to explain again why it cannot be.

I sit in the bedroom I once shared with Catherine and start writing on my blog. It is several hours before I think to check my phone and find that, once again, Lydia has stolen a march on me. Her text is like a fanfare of betrayal:

Guess who's going to be on TV? BBC2. 9pm tomorrow night…Check it out.

It's followed by the usual gush of kisses and emoticons. I know without having to look at the listings which programme she means. I'd been looking forward to the new series. Until now.

'That girl has a chip on her shoulder taller than Oakham Hill; she's always resented being the youngest,' Aunt Philips keeps telling us. She is right of course. Lydia tramples her way through life, making impetuous decision after impetuous decision, almost as if she resolved as soon as she was born that that was the last time she'd come last at anything. She was the first of my sisters to have sex, the first to leave school. The first (and I hope the only one) to get a tattoo. My mother was furious when she saw the pictures Lydia posted on Facebook – two bruise-blue letters on either side of her left wrist, L for Lydia and G for George. Then the first to get married (aged a far from sweet sixteen) and first to have a baby (my beloved niece, Emily). I'm half expecting her to be the first one to get divorced. Perhaps it's just as well that George is stationed overseas for months at a time. Being so often apart seems to have kept them together.

In spite of myself I tune in, strain to hear the show over my mother's constant commentary.

'Doesn't she look beautiful! Who'd have thought it? My Lydia on television – in the Military Wives Choir! Just wait until I tell everyone…'

Somehow I manage to stick it out until the end.

'Is that the time?' I ask, throwing in some exaggerated yawns for good measure. My mother is busy checking for Lydia's name on the list of credits. I leave her to it.

My last is in rhythm but not in blues

Emily's eighth birthday. My mother finds it 'beyond cruel' that she has been denied the opportunity to see her only grandchild on her special day; she seems to hold my father personally responsible for the distance between Newcastle and here. Lydia has posted a photo on Facebook. Typically it's not of the birthday girl herself but one of Lydia. She has had a new tattoo to mark the occasion, adding her daughter's initial. There have been a few responses: a handful of likes and some insipid messages. Only my sister Liz has had the courage to write what we're all thinking.

You do realise it now looks as if you have 'leg' tattooed on your arm?

My father spends most evenings tucked away in his study, listening to Radio 4 on catch-up, or talking to Liz and Jane on Skype. He is on his way there, as if darting to reach cover, when I intercept him. He seems resigned to Lydia's latest stunt.

'Best not goad her. You know how headstrong she can be. She'd probably just get another one. And what with George being a soldier, I wouldn't put it past her to get Army tattooed on her leg.'

'You're incorrigible.' I tell him.

'I think you'll find it's your sister Lydia who is incorrigible.'

I kiss him goodnight.

'I'll be leaving early tomorrow,' I remind him.

'Try not to wake your mother. I'd never hear the end of it.'

I do my best, padding softly down the stairs and closing the door gently behind me. The crisp cobalt sky is deceptive: the first frost has arrived. For a few seconds I hesitate, stand shivering in the chill air, looking back at the house and letting my heels dig into the gravel on the driveway. Then I turn and head off towards the station.

Perhaps the early rounds of auditions were to break us in because this time we all seem resigned to having to wait for hours. My confidence falters as the minutes pass. I start to forget lyrics, start to remember the less charitable jibes my father makes if he feels that I have sung too long. When at last they call my number I want to tell them, 'No. I'm not ready yet. It's far too soon.'

I step out onto the stage platform and squint into the lights. I try not to look at the judges' faces, focus on my feet. I'm asked the standard questions.

'What's your name and where do you come from?'

I push back the impulse to answer with a question of my own or one of those teasing riddles we loved to devise as children: 'My first is in music but not in song.' My mouth feels dust dry and I swallow hard. A few jeers from the crowd break the silence and at last I find my voice.

'My name is Mary Bennet and I'm from Longbourn in Hertfordshire.'

I barely recognise the words I'm saying. I could be talking about a stranger, someone from an unknown place or bygone age. All that is left is the music. I wait for it to start and carry me far from my former self.

CANDOUR

Price W Grisham

There is little doubt (at least among the well-to-do) that virtue is its own reward; yet one hardly need feel guilty if it is occasionally gilded – which it certainly seemed on this golden autumn afternoon, as the esteemed Dr Grant and his wife strolled back towards Mansfield Parsonage. Mrs Grant, grateful to slow her brisker pace to her husband's unsteady one, recalled another very different autumn afternoon, dripping with wet.

Then a much heartier Dr Grant, descrying his patron's delicate niece seeking to screen herself beneath the branches of his wife's newly-planted mulberry tree, had strode out and insisted that she join him, his wife, and her very elegant visiting young sister, in the drawing room. A weaker man, reflected Mrs Grant, might have simply sent out an extra umbrella for her homeward journey; for Miss Price's position in the parish had always been ambiguous.

Although the niece of Sir Thomas and Lady Bertram, Miss Frances Price was not then officially 'out' and, indeed, it seemed, never would be; for she was treated by many in the family – especially Lady Bertram's sister, Mrs Norris – almost as a housemaid. The young lady's modest demeanor, however, had been exquisite. (Not for the first time, Dr Grant had stated calmly concerning his predecessor's widow: 'Mrs Norris, my dear, should be flogged.') Shortly after the Grants' social notice, Miss Price did come out; and sometime later married the younger Bertram son, Edmund.

Ordained, serious, and invariably kind, Edmund Bertram had recently stepped in temporarily to take over Dr Grant's clerical duties, a consequence of the older man's apoplectic attacks. Which would hardly have been the case, Mrs Grant observed sadly, had her ambitious London sister landed Edmund Bertram – especially given the cramped and crumbling parsonage at nearby Thornton Lacey. For there the Bertrams now resided, not rich, but joyful and content in each other's company.

Mrs Grant's mulberry tree had flourished as well, its bounty preserved in pretty glasses resting in her pantry. The good-hearted woman was just beginning to wonder if physical size might correlate *occasionally* to personal kindness – for *they* had always prided themselves on parish hospitality, whereas Mrs Norris (God rest her) had been narrow both in mind *and* body – when her husband broke into her reverie:

'Did I mention that Bramstone's Pemberly pulpit is suddenly opened, my dear? For that excellent man is finally retiring to Bath. So far, the only family connection the Darcys can find for the position is a rather persistent Mr Collins, who does not appear suitable.'

Mrs Grant hid a smile: Dr Bramstone and her husband had been friends at university, where the former had been so apprehensive about his surname forecasting fiery sermons that his pulpit delivery was always icily calm and quite incomprehensible. His congregation, of course, approved: they must surely have a superior padre if he could not be understood.

'My love, I thought it must be soon, given his arthritis in the knees. They cracked so when he mounted the pulpit during our last visit that Mr Bennet – he always nods off, you know – said he thought a French revolutionary had opened fire with a pair of pistols.'

Dr Grant replied, thoughtfully, 'And would he sleep through our friend Edmund's sermons, do you think? For Bertram is never more engaged – and engaging – than when he is in the pulpit, though he is shy outside it: I may say that his reason and earnestness there and his compassion for his parishioners are striking. Yet I think we must consider recommending him, if Sir Thomas approves. Thornton Lacey is not within the Mansfield jurisdiction and the rectory is in ill repair for someone as frail as Fanny – though a hale single man might manage. Their curate, Cooper, seems equal to anything.'

'Ah yes, a very good sort of man, but an Evangelical, you said; his voice a little harsh – not at all like yours; I do think I fell in love first with your voice, my dear.'

So it was that the Hon Edmund Bertram, late of Mansfield and Thornton Lacey parishes, found himself in November newly installed as the vicar of the Pemberley parish. Mr Collins and his good wife Charlotte had been temporarily holding the ecclesiastical fort; and persistent that loquacious priest had been: 'My dear, *dear* Mr Darcy, I brook no refusal; I insist, Lady Catherine insists, even my dear Charlotte insists, that it is my *duty* as a Christian and a clergyman to come to your aid during this propitious – er, this perilous moment.'

Fortunately, Mrs Collins was as sensible (and, Bertram suspected, as gently ironic) as she was plain. She and her husband were to stay at Pemberly a bit longer, where the family were collectively happy to lose Mr Collins either in the expansive greenhouse or the massive library, whilst they provided his patient lady with company and conversation – just as they were now doing, drawn round a crackling fire in a cozy sitting room.

'Mrs Collins, we shall miss you when you return to Lady Catherine; but we do look forward to Mrs Bertram's joining us. She has a brother in the Navy about whose sailings we shall be eager to hear,' ventured Mr Darcy, hoping he had recalled accurately both the brother's profession and the sister's sudden animation. Drawing room conversation was not his strong point; but Mrs Collins was his wife's intimate friend, and he felt kindly toward his new vicar's spouse, whose reticence reminded Darcy of his sister, Georgiana, seated near her.

'Yes, how interesting, indeed!' exclaimed Mrs Collins. 'I wonder often what it might be like to simply sail away – on a journey, I mean. Have you seen your brother's ship, Mrs Bertram? The *Thrush*? Are there ladies travelling aboard?'

'Only Captain Walsh's wife,' Mrs Bertram responded, glancing up from her teacup. 'William says she is kind, and during illnesses, a very skilled nurse.'

Pretty Mrs Darcy, noting that Mr Bertram's wife, like her own husband, preferred listening to speaking, added kindly, 'Mrs Bertram, this mulberry preserve is delicious; do thank Mrs Grant for us. Mr Bertram, did you yourself ever consider the Navy? Or has the Church been your calling from an early age?'

There was a moment's pause. 'Yes, though of course it has few honours or social distinctions. But in no other profession is one able to help at potentially every level, from the poorest cottager to the corridors of White Hall.'

A simultaneous rustle and harrumph sounded from behind

Mr Bennet's newspaper: 'My dear sir... You cannot mean to suggest that ancient holy writ, though perhaps vaguely helpful, has anything to do with modern political or economic structures? If you permit me, I must protest on two grounds: firstly, I cannot possibly think it so; and secondly, I beg you would not introduce any address which causes me to forfeit that Sabbath morning rest to which I have become accustomed – and to which Bramstone's delivery was excellently suited, were it not for his confounded knees. Collins never considers a homily – does he, my dear Charlotte?'

'No, my husband's duties to Lady Catherine leave him little time to compose anything so elaborate as individually prepared remarks,' replied Mrs Collins calmly, successfully avoiding any implication of relief in her voice.

Feeling his way cautiously, Bertram continued: 'Those within a rural parish may not, perhaps, comprehend complex dissertation, whilst wondering whether their winter food supply is adequate; but the deliberation of His Majesty's ministers on how to help struggling families could have an impact on every parish.'

'On that subject, you might indeed gain my wife's ear – a rare commodity, I can assure you,' rejoined Mr Bennet. 'As I have explained to her repeatedly, but never persuasively, the entail of my estate, away from her five daughters to my eternally grateful cousin, is the law. And though it pains me to say so, for reason good: for how else are houses and hamlets to hold together, if one's land and fortune become divided among heaven knows how many children and other livestock?'

'And yet, Papa, such a system certainly limits the potential advancement of young ladies. Had it not been for Mr Darcy and Mr Bingley, you might now be the proud father of two governesses, one paid companion, and possibly a school teacher – all with limited family visitation rights,' replied Mrs Darcy with a smile.

'In such a case, dear Lizzie, I suspect my visits would be limited indeed.'

'I'm afraid I must agree with your father, my dear,' said Mr Darcy, after a slight silence that was becoming awkward. 'The handing down of estates in their entirety to eldest sons not only preserves family land, but the very parish in which it rests: parishes depend on the estate for employment and prosperity.'

'Yet such a system does have its impact on the Church, as well,' Bertram observed, wryly: 'If a younger son has a body too unsound for the military, and an understanding too weak for the law, his only remaining profession is the Church. But did you say you have four sisters, Mrs Darcy? I hope they and Mrs Bennet are well?' Noting Mrs Collins' faint blush, he diverted his remarks with an inner rebuke.

'Yes, she is visiting Mrs Bingley; and with only two daughters for whom to find husbands, is now focusing on a Meryton clerk; she might then keep one daughter at home. Unlike my father, she is not fond of reading and reflection, and must have some company if she is to remain happy.'

'Which has been *my* focus these five-and-twenty years, my dear,' sighed Mr Bennet. 'Look here, Bertram, what ancient passage *could* direct itself to Collins' hapless entailment? If one does exist, he *may* heed it, though I beg you not mention it to Mrs Bennet. She would be pounding down Lord Percival's door directly, and no Prime Minister deserves that.'

'My own reflections, sir, have been on possible legislation concerning the parish poor, some of whom, sadly, may occasionally even come from the very families Mrs Darcy describes. Yet this custom of entailment has often struck me as flawed. For primogeniture itself is not a legal inheritance requirement: it is simply implemented by the purchaser of the estate through long-standing tradition – yet there are few manoeuvres around it. Indeed, Lady Catherine's is the one exception of which I have ever heard.'

The walk back to the Pemberley parsonage soon afterwards was short but sharp with cold; and Bertram's reflections, as he gave a warm and steadying arm to his wife, deepened with the dusk.

'What did you think, my dear? For I could tell that you were listening carefully; your insights would have been welcome to me.'

'Oh! It seemed a gentleman's conversation, surely, though it concerned the fate of nearly every woman in the room. It would have seemed the height of presumption for *me* to comment: not even Mrs Darcy dared continue, though I'm sure she has her own ideas on the subject; how could she not?'

'Well, never think it a presumption to share your thoughts with *me*,' responded her husband with a sad smile. 'Had I heeded them earlier, I might have saved us both pain.'

'Do not say so!' To divert Bertram's mind from those agonising earlier times at Mansfield, she continued: 'I confess that, even before Mr Bennet's inquiry, the situation of his five daughters reminded me of a particular passage in the Old Testament; perhaps in the Book of Numbers; do you recall it?'

'Why…the daughters of Zelophehad…how quick you are!' Bertram exclaimed warmly, adding to himself, 'And how quickly we may need to remove again if I expound upon it…'

Yet a glowing spark in the mind of Sir Thomas' younger son had been struck, and Bertram's wife left him in his study: the basket of mending for the parish poor required her attention.

The sanctuary of St. Michael's was far fuller than usual the following Sunday, as local citizens packed its pews; there were even some from the Methodist chapel. In such a crush, ladies were grateful that narrow gowns no longer required the banning of hoops for maximum seating. The congregation also realised that more bodies meant more warmth, which the distinctly chilly confines of the stone edifice made welcome; but kneeling was not easy.

As he mounted the pulpit steps, Bertram's brow was unfurrowed, yet he could not claim his customary Sabbath serenity. Finally ascended, he looked out over the eagerly murmuring congregation. The elderly sexton had opened the cracked and creaking volume to the passage requested; and drawing a deep breath, the Honourable Reverend Edmund Bertram read, 'From the Book of Numbers, Chapter 21: Moses and the Five Daughters:

'Then came the daughters of Zelophehad…and these are the names of his daughters; Mahlah, and Noah, and Hoglah, and Milcah, and Tirzah. And they stood before Moses, and before

110

Eleazar the priest, and before the princes and all the congregation, *by* the door of the tabernacle of the congregation, saying... Why should the name of our father be done away from among his family, because he hath no son? Give unto us *therefore* a possession among the brethren of our father. And Moses brought their cause before the LORD.And the LORD spake unto Moses, saying, The daughters of Zelophehad speak right: thou shalt surely give them a possession of an inheritance among their father's brethren; and thou shalt cause the inheritance of their father to pass unto them. And thou shalt speak unto the children of Israel, saying, If a man die, and have no son, then ye shall cause his inheritance to pass unto his daughter.'

Mrs Grant examined the late-spring soil around the second mulberry tree she had planted, and looked carefully at its twin, which seemed to have survived another Mansfield winter with little difficulty. No weeds yet – but she could not say the same for herself, she thought, with a wry glance at her black gown. What an odd term for a widow's garb.

'There now,' she said to the handsome new rector and his gentle wife as they all walked together toward the waiting carriage. 'One for Dr Grant; and one for me, for you to remember us by. There is plenty of preserve left, my dears, but Cook has the receipt when you run out.'

Giving them each a kiss, she was then handed into the elegant equipage sent by her sister, and as it rolled away, turned for one last look at the rectory and parish which had been her home for so many happy years. Bertram smiled and raised his hat; Fanny waved her wet handkerchief.

'Don't be weepy,' she told herself sensibly, looking forward again. 'Now that Edmund is returned home from that very peculiar, truncated time at Pemberly, you know he will take *good* care of all the families around Mansfield.'

And for more than forty years, the Honourable Reverend Edmund Bertram, and his faithful Fanny, did.

FIVE THEORIES

Leslie McMurtry

My statement? I'd prefer to share my theories and see which one makes the most sense to you.

1. That a lady had been attacked.

As I've said once, and I don't mind repeating, I have a handcart. It's the time of morning when no one but the milk floats are out. You'll remember it was raining two nights ago. The road was filthy. My mother gets very cross with me, you see, if I track dust from the road into the bakery. Yes, it is relevant. I was sleepy on account of not having a good night's rest, the night before. Early rising doesn't usually affect me. It's the time of year when the sun will wake you if you leave even a peep of a curtain open.

Because I was sleepy, I didn't notice right away when I left the bakery that I'd forgotten the Chelsea buns. My route takes me past Mrs Maheer, no. 3, and she always has a Chelsea bun. Regular as clockwork. I've been in the neighbourhood with my handcart since the year of the Accession, and it's always been this way. I was paused, then, in front of the station, already late and deciding what to do.

There is a little grassy bank opposite the station – you know it. I just happened to look towards it and saw a woman standing there. She was dressed in white, and I could tell at that distance that she was rather more old than young. She hadn't a hat or a coat on. She was standing, but after a few moments I was unsure what she was looking at. As if she was reading the lettering above the ticket hall over and over: Crofton Park, Crofton Park, Crofton Park.... Therefore I called out to her. My beckoning call had no effect. I rolled my handcart as near up the knoll as I could, waiting to see if the lady would make any sign that she'd seen or heard me.

The lady's mute condition led me to believe she was suffering from some fit. As I drew closer, I saw that the lady's age was very advanced. I would have thought her not younger than seventy, though she had the gravity of a gentlewoman. Perhaps she was frightened to be approached by a baker's assistant in workman's clothes, with mud – unfortunately – all over his shoes. 'Madam?' I said softly, so as not to alarm her.

'I beg your pardon?' she returned. At this moment, her eyes, contemplating fixedly, as I have said, the entrance to the station, lighted upon me.

'Are you quite all right, ma'am?'

'I think so,' she said. She held out her hand for me to assist her down the grassy bank. She was wearing no gloves, and her skin was very pale and rather blue. Her hair was white and neatly pinned. She was wearing proper clothes, not night-clothes. 'Do you know who I am?' she asked.

2. That the lady had hit her head.

I did not know by what accident the lady had lost her memory. I could see no evidence of a blow to the head. She still clung to my hand; her pulse was quick as a bird's. 'I don't, I'm afraid,' I said, honestly.

'Is that cart yours?' she asked.

'Yes,' I said.

'I think I am a hostess of an hotel,' she said.

'Oh really? Which one?' I brightened at the thought of reuniting her with her family or friends. The nearest thing to a hotel which I could bring to mind was Mrs Curtis' lodgings at 278, New Cross Road. I proposed to take the lady there.

'I ride the stagecoach and provide services at hotels along the route.'

I thought this is a bit queer, but it was possible the woman was a foreigner who had been separated from her touring companions. Still I persisted in asking her to which hotel I should convey her.

'No . . . that's my second cousin,' she said. She was looking very confused, and I was at my wit's end. 'My cousin is American,' she went on, perfectly oblivious to the situation. 'She writes me letters, but now I know, *she* is the Harvey Girl. But I cannot remember...'

'Do you remember where you live?' I asked her. I admit I was tiring of the situation and thinking Mrs Maheer would scold me for being late. 'Or perhaps you know the address of your doctor?'

The lady was unable to give me any positive answers, and so I suggested I take her to the nearest police station. After some deliberation, she agreed. She was not agitated, as the elderly sometimes are in such moments. She seemed neither weary nor uncomfortable. We proceeded to the police station. I wheeled my cart, and she followed. As we went, she spoke: 'I think it is clear now. My name is Eleanor Tilney. We must look for my brother, Henry. Do you know him?'

I must have manifested my confusion in a frown; it was an uncommon name, but there were many people in the area. 'What is his business?'

'Oh, he has none, he is a gentleman. My elder brother is in the Army.'

I mentioned the barracks at Woolwich Arsenal.

'If we are in London, they will all be staying in Grosvenor Park with my father.'

That Mrs, or Miss, or Lady Tilney was in some doubt made me fear she was being whimsical. 'And where else, if not in London?'

'Bath, of course. Our home is at Northanger Abbey. Do you know it?'

'I think we had better go to the police station first, ma'am.'

'Of course,' she murmured. Then a few moments later, 'That is my mother.'

'Who is?'

'My mother was Eleanor Tilney. That was her maiden name. She met my father somewhat later in life, owing to the fact there was great family tragedy in her youth. She loved her brother, and her brother's wife. I hardly knew them... Ah, I see. I was dreaming about her last night.'

3. That the lady had been sleep-walking.

The unknown lady in whose family tree there was evidently a Tilney seemed distressed by the realisation that – well, either that her mother was long dead, that Northanger Abbey had long passed out of the family, that she was a spinster living somewhere nearby; any of these notions could be the logical catalyst. I begged her leave to hail a hansom to take her to the police station as it would take us several more minutes on foot. She refused. I heard the milk float approaching and hoped that the driver would assist me with the confused lady.

However, shortly before the driver was within hailing distance, the lady said, 'Yes, yes, of course. Number 36, Hazeldon Road.' With surprising certainty, she turned and began walking there. I followed, with the handcart. This, of course, took us back to Crofton Park Station.

The indicated number 36 seemed a modest property from the front. The lady turned the latch, and the door opened. I proposed to stay no longer than necessary to make sure she had found the correct residence. I now had her address and could ask a policeman and a clergyman to check on her and see if she had any relatives. The silence of the flat as she opened the door indicated there was no other living soul within. I peeked inside, satisfied it was an ordinary residence. 'Come in,' she said as she disappeared into the front parlour. 'I must thank you, young man, for helping me.'

I told her it was not necessary and that I could not leave my cart, which would in any case not fit through the doorway. She emerged, holding within her hands a collar of the most stunning diamonds I had ever seen in my life. Not paste-board: real diamonds. 'It was my mother's,' she said. She held it out to me, then snatched it back. 'Come in, there is more,' she said.

4. That the lady was mad.
Fearing that the lady might come to some mischief in the neighbourhood, flashing jewels like that about, I hesitantly followed her into the rather cold and dark flat. It seemed unlikely that the lady had any coal in the grate. I saw no electricity to brighten the gloom but turned up a convenient oil lamp. There was, however, no squalor, for everything was kept in sparkling order. There was, indeed, on a low table a stack of letters in a girlish hand postmarked from a variety of locations in the American West; on the wall was a large oval portrait of a very beautiful woman of the eighteenth century, I think – I am no expert on art – wearing white and fashionably attired. Diamonds shone from her ears.

The lady displayed the diamond necklace and rings and earrings to match it. I was speechless but resolved to calm the lady down, put her to bed, and call immediately for a doctor. To that end, I told her that I would agree to take whatever she wanted to give me. But would she have a cake from the cart? She said she would and entered the scullery in order to make a pot of tea.

She was a remarkable lady, for all her vagueness of mind, and had evidently led an interesting life of nearly a century's length, if the woman in the portrait was indeed her mother. It had been impossible to tell if there was any family resemblance.

5. That the lady had committed foul deeds.

No, I cannot explain the blood on my shirt-sleeves. I suppose it must be my own. I cannot remember being cut. The lady had a letter-opener on the table next to her correspondence.

Do I recall anything after the lady had left for the scullery? I was admiring her bookshelves. I remember chasing off some boys who ought to have been on their way to school from thieving from my cart. Fearful that the noise would disturb the lady, I closed the front door.

Did I notice that the clock needed winding? No – did it?

BENWICK'S TALE

Eithne Cullen

I can honestly say that up till that stay in Lyme, I had only really loved three people. Frederick Wentworth was my dearest friend, mentor and companion. We were the keenest young officers who served in the navy, seeking out battles with Napoleon's fleet. Then there was Harville, who was like a brother to me. We were reckless but willing: learning well our skills, so that now all three of us are captains; all have made our fortune.

My third love was Fanny.

On leave, in those early days, we all fell in love. Harville married Jane, the lovely girl he had known since childhood. They settled in a modest cottage and started a family. It was an act of faith, no one knew if he would live or die in battle, or whether they would be poor throughout their marriage.

In contrast, Frederick had his heart almost broken. He loved a girl, I believe it was true and deep affection between them. Her family held her back, stopped her taking the risk that he would, one day, make the fortune needed to marry a baronet's daughter. Frederick cut all ties, he carried the hurt around with him. Even when he took home Spanish gold as bounty, he did not return to her, write to her or mention her name.

Harville welcomed me into his world, and I met Fanny, his sister. She moved with the grace and elegance of the finest lady; her voice was soft and lyrical. We shared a love of poetry and talked for hours. She could draw and sing; her needlework was fine and delicate. I adored her; I begged her to enter into an engagement immediately. With another war on the horizon, I hesitated, my family was not wealthy. I asked Fanny to wait for me, we made a pledge and I went off to war.

I was at sea when I heard that she was sick; Admiral Croft's wife joined us at Lisbon. She'd travelled over-land to catch up with the convoy, and she told me of the fever Fanny had contracted. She was by the sea, now, with Harville's wife, the air was said to be good for her lungs. She was positive that Fanny would recover and be strong again. My fortune was secure – now, we might live a comfortable life. My ship, the *Grappler*, was heading for the Cape. It would be two months before I was home in Portsmouth. My heart was heavy with the fear.

There was another difficulty to face. Harville had caught some shot in the last skirmish we'd been in. Mrs Croft had been shocked by his appearance, saying he looked older than Wentworth and me, though we are all the same age. He was sent home to rest and recover from his illness.

Wentworth went back, too, and was given a huge welcome sailing into Plymouth where he received the news that Fanny had died. Being the friend he is, being the man for whom I feel such love, such loyalty, he headed to Portsmouth to await my return. Wentworth knew he had to be the one to tell me, he knew Harville's heart would break. He knew I would not be fit to bring my crew in safely when I heard the news. Arriving in the port, he took a small rowing boat and came to meet the ship, boarded and came to me. He talked of Fanny: her beauty, talents, warmth and kindness. He shared my abject sorrow and aching hurt. He stayed with me a full week, talking to me, comforting me, wiping my tears. My ship sailed back to port under Frederick's orders. We did not leave the ship till he knew I was able to face the sight of land, of home and my dear friend, Harville. I can never say how much he meant to me, why Harville and I hold him so dear.

That autumn passed in so much pain. I was out of sorts with my family and friends. I paced at night, sleepless and unsettled. I read all day, brooding over the words of sad poems that matched my mood, such as Byron's 'And thou art dead, as young and fair As aught of mortal birth; And form so soft, and charms so rare, Too soon return'd to Earth!'

Harville was slowly recovering, his loss of his sister and his frail health took their toll on him. I was delighted when he wrote to me that he and the family were to rent a cottage in Lyme for six months; they asked me to join them. It suited us all, we had warmth and companionship; we had the sea and shoreline to walk on for hours on end.

One day, Frederick Wentworth arrived to surprise us. It turned out

124

that he was staying just seventeen miles from us, in a country house. Time turned back for us, three friends together at last. The emptiness in my heart was there, like a void, but the friendship cheered me. Harville's wife commented that Frederick had done us both good and begged him to stay or come again soon. That evening we talked and laughed about days we had shared, life in the Navy and our deep and valuable friendship. Harville seemed to brighten, too; we all knew Wentworth's visit had been like a tonic to us.

When he told the Musgroves, the friends he was visiting, they insisted on returning with him and quickly arranged carriages, luggage and lodgings. He arrived with two young women, their brother – a foppish but likeable man – and his wife, Mary, who had left behind her children in order to restore her health. Mary's sister, Anne was the last member of the party. Harville and I quickly realised that she was *the* Anne Elliott, Wentworth's longed-for bride from years ago.

I felt tired and ill-at-ease; and wished for quiet and time to think. The younger girls were chatting and giggling; fascinating and annoying at the same time. Wentworth watched them with interest, we realised he was looking for a wife. Louisa, bright and pretty, tried to attract his attention all the time.

I fell into step with Anne Elliott; at once, I realised the gentle appeal of this bright, educated and sympathetic woman. She must be almost thirty but she had a girlish air about her, a simple beauty. I was startled by her directness; she brought up the subject of Fanny's death and expressed her understanding of my sad state. We walked and talked; for the first time in many months I felt at ease in the company of someone new.

That evening, at dinner, I sought out Miss Elliott, once more, and engaged in conversation with her. I was delighted to find her so well read, wise and thoughtful in her speech. Anne listened to me for some time; I was surprised by her change of tone when she encouraged me to read less sad verse and some more uplifting prose. We both laughed: I knew I had been given sound advice I would resist, she knew she'd had her say whether I take the advice or not.

125

Next morning, the visitors lingered, not too eager to head off home. A last walk on the Cobb was proposed. We all went happily. Surprisingly, I found myself musing upon the women in our party. Mary and Henrietta walked nearest us; Mary lecturing her sister-in-law upon the unsuitability of her suitor; Henrietta, without her sibling, an obedient listener. Neither of these held my attention; these types I had often seen.

I watched Harville and Anne, deep in conversation. She held my interest; most like myself of all the party, with the earnestness and gravity that others recognised in me. If I were ever to love again, could this be the sort of woman who would be a companion? I strained to listen to their conversation; it was with a flash of guilt that I heard they were bantering about who loved most constantly: man or woman. She presented her case well, and I wondered if she were talking of herself and Frederick. After all, she must have had other offers, she was a worthy match from a good family.

Hearing the girlish laughter of the younger Musgrove girl, I recognised many of the qualities I had loved in Fanny: her lilting voice, her infectious laughter, the lightness of her step and the way she looked directly at Wentworth as she spoke to him.

Anne's words about men's inconstancy suddenly pulled me back to myself; Fanny was only five months dead.

What happened next was pure foolishness. Louisa, intent on flirting with Frederick, was jumping from the steps of the Cobb squealing: 'Catch me!' Frederick did catch her, but I could see he was uncomfortable; the steps were high, the ground beneath our feet wet and slippery, there was not much room to move. She turned, flying up the steps, calling: 'Again, again!' Real concern came into Wentworth's voice: 'Louisa, no. Stop there! Don't!'

She did not listen, launching herself, squealing with delight towards his arms. He did not catch her, despite his best efforts. To all our horror, she lay, still and unconscious close to his feet. Panic filled the company. I cannot remember who said what, or which of the ladies screamed or cried. I saw Harville freeze in terror and Musgrove's face crumple in sorrow. Only Anne, calm, sensible Anne,

126

moved with purpose. She lifted Louisa's head and put her shawl under it. Wentworth, used to taking a frigate into battle against Napoleon's fleet, froze to the spot and stammered. 'A surgeon!' she commanded. Wentworth rose to his feet; 'Not you: Benwick, he knows where to find one!' She instructed Wentworth to take Louisa to the inn. Looking at Louisa, I wondered if Fanny had been like this at the end, when the fever would not leave her body. I hurried away.

By the time I arrived with the surgeon, they were settled at the inn. Anne was clearly the one in control, and my admiration for her grew. However, it was to Louisa that my heart turned, this helpless little bird, broken on the bed. I felt a resurgence of the sorrow I had felt for Fanny. A voice inside my head told me that if Louisa lived she would need a protector – might that be me? I withdrew into myself and observed the chaos as it turned to calm; the one who orchestrated the calm was the quiet woman with sense and feeling. Frederick was ashen, shocked to the core, I knew he was blaming himself for Louisa's state.

It was suggested that the Uppercross party should go to tell Louisa's parents of the accident. Mary's shrill cry pierced the room, filled the inn. She should stay, Anne was not even family. Anne complied, though everyone knew she was most able to care for Louisa. I realised this was the problem that had blocked Wentworth's hopes of marriage all those years ago, how compliant Anne was, always the one to keep the peace: a strength or a fault? She left with Wentworth.

The surgeon said Louisa had suffered a head injury, all we could do was wait, ensure she did not contract a fever and pray. We stayed like this for several days. The Musgroves arrived, her mother and father: such warm and loving parents. I could see they suppressed their irritation at Mary's wish to draw attention to herself all the time. I think it was when I saw their love for Louisa, their real familial love, that I knew I wanted to be closer to her.

We took Louisa back to Harville's cottage and settled into a much calmer way of life for the following weeks. Louisa slept, though we became aware of her eyes opening and taking in the scene. I often sat and read to her, I knew she was listening and would sometimes see her expression change.

Harville and his wife watched me and saw my growing affection for Louisa; I begged them not to think me fickle or disloyal to Fanny's memory. They did not expect any more from me than to remember Fanny as my first love.

By the time Louisa was well, I loved her dearly. We talked, we walked – tentatively at first – down to the Cobb. There was no more ill-advised jumping. She learned to like the poems that I liked, she sat with Jane Harville in the evenings, drawing or sewing. She sometimes longed for a dance or a ball and we promised there would be time for that when she was fully recovered.

Wentworth, now, became less guilty about his part in Louisa's accident. He watched her closely when he visited, looking for signs of injury. She teased him, not as she had flirted with him before, she knew his worry and concern were real. She looked on him as a kindly uncle or brother, now. He saw that he was under no obligation to her. There was no expectation of an engagement. I could see his relief; I do not think he could see mine.

When we were alone, I asked after Anne. He thought perhaps I might have formed some attachment to her after our deep conversations during her visit. I assured him that I looked forward to meeting her again to continue a friendship, but no more.

I spoke to both my friends about my intention to marry Louisa. I think Harville thought it was too soon after Fanny's death, a year had not passed. Though he had seen me sad for too long, now. Frederick was happy for me, that I could laugh again. I wished he could find some happiness, too. I asked if he had given up any plans to find a wife; he surprised me with some comment about how he had tried to look around for a wife, but always came back to one thought, one woman worthy of his affections. Little did I know that her constancy matched his; he could find happiness after these long years.

We travelled to Uppercross to share our news and wedding plans, and met delight and approval. Though Mary Musgrove was not gushing in her praise. I understood she was not so happy in the girls' choices of husbands: a poor country clergyman and a sea captain with no family to talk of.

Wedding plans were under way for both the sisters.

'Do you not want to go to Bath?' I asked her.

'I am more settled here,' she replied.

The Harvilles were as surprised as I, that she would choose our quiet life above the thrill of shopping and assemblies. They exchanged amused glances at her response.

'Mother can do all that for me,' she laughed, 'All that nonsense about weddings and which warehouses to visit, a lot of fuss over nothing. Benwick dear, do you mind if we just stay here?'

I had no intention of going to Bath to look at cloths and ribbons. I was pleased and surprised that Louisa chose to remain with me in the quiet of the country-side. I knew she truly wanted to be with me: the thrill of Bath, of dancing and society could wait. We would go there, soon, to enjoy the season as Captain and Mrs Benwick, after all there was a whole lifetime ahead of us.

FAREWELL LADY CATHERINE

Fiona Skepper

Anne took her mother's hand, and uncurled her fingers one by one, counting on her limp, bent digits.

The palm had remained smooth but the back was oversized and wrinkled, with a few scars and blemishes, despite years of assiduous glove wearing, and it stood out starkly against the pale, tiny bed of her daughter's ten fingers. They were as different as a mountain and a snowflake, in more ways than hands, mused Anne. The hand she held had once gesticulated strongly, gripped her shoulder, and had indicated its approval and disapproval with the slightest tilt. She had idolised and been terrified of the hand, as she had its bearer.

Anne started at the beginning.

One: the thumb. 'It's half the size of the rest. Short like me. Remember when I was small and you tried your best to strengthen me with that tonic you made me drink. When was it you became convinced that it would do me good? You fully advocated its use for many different ills, and for many different recipients. Even when I came of age you made Mrs Jenkinson stand over me and watch me swallow. Do you know Mamma, I am still not able to eat alone without feeling that eyes are boring into me, checking I have first consumed the tonic. No wonder I've always had problems keeping food down.

'Despite my careful obedience to your instructions, I did not thrive. However although I possessed an inability to play like other children, I had the expected reveries of a young girl. I dreamed of the handsome prince who would come and save me. You didn't know of course, you didn't enquire into my daydreaming, hence it is strange that it was you, Mamma, who fulfilled my wish, in a way at least. You gave me a prince, you gave me Fitzwilliam. For as long as I can remember you told me that I would be his, and be mistress of Pemberley. You left me that vision to fill my empty days, and it did. Even with your great insight, Mamma, I'm not sure if you realised that you face a difficulty when attempting to rid yourself of some childhood dreams. They cling.'

Two: the index finger. 'People would point Fitzwilliam out when he came in to a room. "There is Mr Darcy," little more had to be said.

So handsome my heart would always flutter and beat faster. He said very little to me, and seemed annoyed by the responses I gave. I felt like a fool around him. I admit I feared him but I also loved him because you told me to. I believed then that the world was as you directed. Novels fill young girls with silly ideas; young people should be seen and not heard; the weather tomorrow will be what you say; Anne will be Mrs Darcy.'

Three: the middle finger. 'Yours is perfect. Mine fails in comparison, of course. Do you remember I used to bite this nail on my left hand? You complained I did it all the time, but I only did it when I was afraid. You held up your hand as an example of a proper appendage. You ordered the maid to paint soap on my nail every day until I ceased to interfere with it. I did of course. I felt ashamed and I would always place my right hand over my left when I was without gloves, so others couldn't see my sin. I let myself be covered in your protective mantle, all decisions were yours. I voiced no opposition or complaint. I obeyed the commandment to honour my mother. I fell silent immediately when you raised this hand, with all its perfect fingers, ever so slightly. I patiently kept my own counsel and expected my reward.'

Four: the ring finger. 'You have the proof that you have achieved the ambition of all women, a beautiful gold band from my father.'

Anne held up a blank hand. 'You can see mine is still empty, when we both thought that by now I would be ringed and dispatched. I can't complain for want of preparedness. You gave me strict and detailed lessons regarding my housekeeping duties. You instructed me on how I was to treat servants, organise accounts and entertain guests, although you knew I possessed no talent at performing any of these basic requirements. I tried so hard though to take note of everything you said. I've imagined this hand with a ring for so long. At my heart's core was my vision of the future when I would be sent away from you.'

Five: the little finger. 'When the poison first crept in, a word here, a rumour there, you laughed and said it was a ridiculous calumny. You took my hand then, and declared I had more nobility and breeding in my smallest finger, than in Miss Bennet's entire family. Then the skies darkened. You came home from your visit, and barely said a word that whole evening. I was terrified. However, the next day you ranted and raved, telling me horror stories about their crassness and vulgarity; her youngest sister, without honour or virtue, disgraced herself with a steward's son. I breathed deeply. The world was set right. You took away my distress, as how could Fitzwilliam want to spend a minute in such company?

'I did not realise then of course, that as much as you relieved my fears, you did not relieve you own. How could I have recognised that undiscovered country? I had never witnessed you truly afraid before.

'Do you realise what you risk when you shatter a dream? It's a dangerous thing to do. The moment that you told me that the door that leads to Pemberley was shut, it was strange but something broke inside me, like a spring inside the clock on the mantel that was sent to the servant's room. Did you know, Mama, that I ran to the balcony on the top floor and thought about throwing myself off? What a disgrace to the ancient name of de Bourgh that would have been! Then the most peculiar thing happened, I felt the pride of my ancestors rising inside me, something I had never experienced before in all my sickly existence. And I found that the most predominant feeling was anger. I should explain, it was not wild anger, I have always remembered that I am a lady and I did not desire to throw objects around the room. What I desired most was justice. On reflection, I found in some ways it was strangely liberating. My search for justice passed over Fitzwilliam and the Bennet girl as, to give them their due, I realised they never made vows to me, they never betrayed me. As I tried to order the feelings of my heart further, I realised that the events that broke my bond to Fitzwilliam miraculously also seemed to have broken my bond to you.'

A sudden surge of feeling rushed through Anne, she squeezed the old hand so hard that she thought she spied a slight spasm on the wizened, still face, and a small noise came from the parched old lips…
'Haaa…' Anne leaned over her mother, her face close to hers, all restraint suddenly gone.

135

'You lied to me Mamma, you lied. Fitzwilliam will never be mine; he never desired to be mine. I realised too late that it was all silly fancy on your part, you weren't all-powerful. In fact you were weak. You were too weak to make it happen.'

Anne was almost on top of her mother now, pinning her wrists down on her bed with what strength she possessed. A crumpled face of fear looked back at her. Surprised, Anne loosened her grip, sat back down, but continued to keep Lady Catherine's hand in hers and stared at the shrivelled figure for some time. Eventually, a tiny smile appeared at the corner of Anne's mouth.

Anne felt a hand on her arm. It was Mrs Jenkinson.

'It's not good for you to sit so long with her, Miss. Come and rest.'

'No.' said Anne. Both she and Mrs Jenkinson were surprised at the forcefulness with which she said it.

'Forgive me Mrs Jenkinson, I wish to spend as much time as I can by her bedside.'

'Of course, Miss. Is there anything I can get you?' Mrs Jenkinson asked in her usual soothing manner.

Anne just shook her head.

Mrs Jenkinson hesitated. 'I know Doctor Lamb has explained to you, there's no chance. We are just waiting for when the good Lord sees fit—'

'Stop, please, don't speak of it…' Anne turned away. Her shoulders heaved and shook; her handkerchief fluttering around the area of her face.

Mrs Jenkinson was disconcerted by this strange show of emotion from her usually taciturn charge.

'I'll leave you alone.' She hurried out of the room.

Anne leaned back and sighed. She rubbed her dry eyes. She went over to the window surveying the park below.

Anne turned and sat down on the edge of the bed again.

'It is strange isn't it, but I think I have said more to you these last few minutes than I have my entire three-and-twenty years. I am attempting to emulate some of your praiseworthy frankness. I know I'm a little late, at my age, but before my focus had been turned north to another great house and I saw nothing but my future with him.

'There are so many matters to discuss. Here I am, Mohammed has had to come to the mountain, just as the mountain is crumbling into ruin, and for the first time you must hear all.

'Was it the pollution you had to swallow when you went and saw Fitzwilliam with that Bennet girl that has now made you bedridden? It must have been very difficult I know, especially after you swore fervently to anyone for miles, that you would never present yourself there again. I believed you, Mamma, and welcomed your support. However you had a change of heart. I think I may have been able to forgive you but for this last act of betrayal. I suppose I shouldn't blame you for finding it impossible to keep away from Fitzwilliam. For me, the separation feels like a limb has been severed.'

Anne turned her face to the window again.

'You should not be troubled, however. It is not that I face a lifetime of spinsterhood if I choose not to. Despite my weak constitution I have discovered I have talents that have made me so attractive to the opposite sex that I have as many suitors lining up as Penelope did in mythical Ithaca. Do you recall how Mr Collins said, with his mouth full of tea and cake, that I am charming, and my health has "deprived the British court of its brightest ornament". You stated that my features showed my high birth, but that's not quite the same as saying I am a beauty, like they said of the Bennet girl. You told people that I have a wonderful ear for music and would have been very proficient a performer if my health had allowed, as I would have been a good horsewomen, and good dancer, and lady-in-waiting to the Queen, all but for my health. However there is no need to despair as I have discovered I have the quality that makes a sickly constitution beautiful; that of being the heiress to a great fortune. I now know it is the sole reason why anyone will ever profess affection for me.'

Anne's voice began to quiver at this point, she began to shake, and tears flowed down her face breaking her heretofore composed countenance.

'Oh, Mamma. Why did you not just strangle my sick, feeble body in my cradle?'

Anne threw herself on her mother in a tearful embrace, holding her for a few moments, and sobbing quietly.

A noise then broke the silence, soft and incoherent at first, but then getting louder, as though coming from the very depths of the soul of the body on the bed. 'Hhee...Hel...Help me. Help.'

Anne then let go and stood up, wiping her eyes, and looked around furtively, but there was no sound from the corridor, and Anne exhaled.

'As you will see I am far more considerate in my attentions to you.'

Anne picked up one of the large feather pillows edged in a lace, which lay on the grand bed. She knew her puny strength would prove inadequate, so she laid her whole body on it, as it lay on Lady Catherine's once handsome features. She continued to lay there some time after all movement or struggle beneath ceased. She just wanted to sleep, close to her mother, right there, for a long time. Anne knew this could not be, however, and she was one who accepted the inevitable. She stood up, replaced the pillow, straightened her attire, and returned to sitting by the bedside. She kissed her mother's open palm with her cold lips. Then she let go and Lady Catherine's limp arm flopped down on top of her now lifeless body.

'Goodbye Mamma.'

ROMANCE AND REHYDRATION

Sarah Shaw

A few men answered my ad on the dating site, maybe because I said I was looking for fun and friendship: my sister Kitty told me later that 'fun' can be code for casual sex. One or two kept texting.

I agreed to meet Michael near the statue of the mermaid for a seaside walk. My sister Lizzie dropped me off. The guy standing next to the mermaid looked younger than me, with dark hair.

'Lydia? I hope you don't mind the rain,' he said.

'I'll be fine. I feel like a Teletubby, I've got so many layers on.' I introduced the layers because I didn't want him to reject me as too fat.

We strolled along the promenade. Waves rolled in with white crests, the grey sky spat and an excavator moved shingle.

'I love storms,' he said.

He was walking close enough for his hand to brush mine, in order for me to hear him over the crash of breakers.

'I used to come here on holiday when I was a kid,' he continued. 'I remember climbing out the window one night. The thunder boomed, the lightning and the lighthouse flashed. Indoors it bothered me so I couldn't sleep, but outside it felt exciting.'

A romantic. He used the f-word: felt.

When he asked about my job I cringed inside because my ex-husband, George, always said I could do better. Rather than sales assistant, I said, 'I'm a beauty consultant. I give women makeovers and help them to feel good about themselves.'

'My job's with young offenders, trying to get them to avoid committing any more crimes.'

He cared about people. Imagining all those young men cut adrift from their moorings as they wallowed towards Michael for rescue, I wanted to ask him straight away whether he'd be interested in reclaiming me. But it was essential to stay cool and friendly on a first date. I wondered whether I was smiling too much.

We drank hot chocolate on the pier and then returned to the mermaid, where I met Lizzie; she'd popped in to visit our oldest sister, Jane.

'He didn't look good enough for you,' she said.

141

'In what way?'

'He looked a bit greasy.'

'It's the rain. Even the mermaid looks greasy.'

I wondered if I was too old for him, too dried up. When I got home, he texted:

Wow u r really somethin lydia. Cliche list as follows, very attractive intelligent empathetic, a lover of life and the beautiful world. Hope u r up 4 meeting again, Michael.

He seemed perfect: not playing games but letting me know right away that he liked me. But when I texted about going out for a meal and he suggested a boat trip from Orford the following Sunday, I had to wonder why he was avoiding an evening date. I dismissed the suspicion that he might be married and sent him my home address.

On Sunday morning he picked me up in his Renault.

'I saw a movie last night with my sister. You do anything interesting?' I asked when we set off.

'My son always stays over on Friday and Saturday nights. He's eight. His mother… We've been divorced for three years.'

'That's a shame.' A child provided a reassuring excuse for Saturday evenings.

'I'd like him to meet you some time. But I don't want to rush into anything. He's the most important person in my life.'

'My two are grown up.' They used to be my most important people but I needed to let go.

On the boat we ate brunch in a cramped cabin, a middle-aged couple among other couples except that we smiled and talked more than most. A girl in an apron placed half a glass of orange juice in front of me and offered a Cava bottle. 'Buck's Fizz, Madam?'

'Lovely.'

'I'm driving.' Michael placed his hand over his glass.

Outside, the strip of deck that edged the cabin forced us to stand close together. We watched the estuary glide by and commented on dilapidated military installations. When a passing stranger pressed me against Michael, I felt something bubble up, hope or desire, so that I wanted him to touch me more thoroughly and begin my

142

rehydration. At home, I invited him in for a cup of tea. We sat in the garden.

'It hasn't rained for a week. I can't believe I've already had to use the hose,' I said.

'Let's hope it's a hot summer.' He looked at his watch. I wanted to stroke the dark hairs on his arm. 'I'd better go.'

He kissed me on the lips. A shower of rain on earth so parched it had split into scabs that curled up round the edges in a crazy-paving pattern.

That evening he sent a text:

I am an alcoholic i drink a bottle of vodka a day. Need you 2 know love Michael.

So that's why he avoided evenings. Shock and pity stopped me dead. All the times I practised lifesaving on George when he was doing too much coke or speed, hauled him up from the sewer or floated him through hangovers. Drink and drugs turned into a swamp where nothing lovely grew, only swamp grass that cut my hand, stinging flies and mosquitoes. I couldn't live in that quagmire because it sucked me down, and nearly drowned me in the end. Only one kiss with Michael and already I felt confused.

'Don't meet him again, even if you like him,' Lizzie told me. 'You need someone without so many complications.'

The second guy arranged to meet me at a bar in town. When I arrived it seemed embarrassing to be scanning all the men in the place.

'Are you Lydia?' Like a badger, Ralph had a long nose with a squared tip, while his hair was dark grey, streaked white above his brows. His body looked baggy under a good suit, with a bit of a paunch. He bought me a glass of Rioja and I told him a joke about a nun on a merchant ship.

He laughed. 'I love a woman with a sense of humour.'

He invested in construction. He owned a boat and offered to teach me to sail. He invited me for a meal. We shared a squid-with-chilli-and-garlic starter, which made me happy because so many people are repelled by squid.

143

'Have you travelled a lot?' He slathered butter on the last of the bread after the waitress removed our plates.

'I flew to Australia when my sister Mary got married. That's the furthest I've been. How about you?'

The woman returned immediately with our main courses. As I slid my wineglass out of the way I noticed his gaze locked on her breasts. A debatable majority of men can't control their eyes; it meant nothing.

'I lived in Botswana for a while, after I left uni. I worked on a project financed by voluntary organisations to help with agriculture.' He sawed a chunk off one of his venison sausages.

I drew him out about the project: not only developing a variety of millet that could grow in three inches of rainfall but also irrigation.

'What, like wells and pumps?'

'Mostly polythene pit dams, where you trap storm waters in a deep pit lined with polythene.'

He was *perfect*. He could trap my storm waters so they'd keep me moist through the dry season.

Sensing my enthusiasm, he looked directly into my eyes. 'I'm good with my hands.'

My appetite disappeared. If I found a good man who could rehydrate me I wouldn't eat for comfort but transform into a slender, self-confident woman. I took a taxi home on my own because I didn't want to rush into anything while I was pissed. When he rang my mobile the following day, I found myself laughing and heading upstairs for better reception.

On our next date we walked along the quayside to look at his boat.

'If you hold on to this rail with the other hand, you can step across easily. Even wearing sexy heels,' he said. His flirting, though it embarrassed me, also made me feel desirable. He showed me where he cooked and where he slept.

'We could have a little lie down now, before supper.' He was laughing.

'Not gonna happen.'

'You could come when I cross the Channel next weekend. Think about it.'

When he nudged his arm beneath mine as we strolled through the warm, dank smell of the harbour, his knuckles made the side of my breast tingle.

'I hope you don't mind, but I said I'd meet this couple who crew for me in races. Just for one drink,' he said.

The man was Dutch, about the same age as Ralph but lean and brown. The woman looked a lot younger; she had shiny hair and smooth skin. Ralph bought a round. I gradually noticed that he was directing all his questions and remarks to the young woman: he mirrored her body language, crossing his legs when she crossed hers and reaching for his pint when she took a sip; he replaced his glass on the table so that it touched hers. I began to count the number of times Ralph looked at her and compared it with the frequency of his glances at me. Even though I estimated that he was giving her eighty per cent of his attention, I couldn't complain, since I had no right to his desire or esteem. But if this was only our second date, what would happen once we'd been together five years and he'd already had the fun of digging a pit, lining it with polythene and splashing around in my storm waters?

George was a flirt. After I fell for his charm I loved him for his good nature and his underwater skills. But I found out that when he'd claimed to be on an instructorship training course in Gibraltar with the Army Sub-Aqua Association, he'd lied. The photos on his phone showed a woman I'd never met, naked on a bed, and I knew that my husband had been diving her fresh water. We had the kids by then and I stayed with him too long so they wouldn't lose their father. After that I wanted a man who was prepared to devote all his hydraulics to me.

Ralph laughed when the young woman said something that wasn't even funny. I escaped to the loo, where I texted Jane: Pls fone me x.

Back at the table, answering her call, I exclaimed, 'Oh my God. I'll come straight away!' I stood and slipped my arms into my jacket. 'Sorry, got to go.'

I arrived home too exhausted for a shower.

I met Gabe at Jane's party. Outside the house, while we watched sparks from a bonfire jet into the night, we ended up discussing our favourite movies.

'I'd like to see you again.' His Derbyshire accent reminded me of George, whose voice I loved so much that I used to save his messages on my answerphone even after we separated.

I fumbled for my phone. 'Tell me your number. No, hang on, I've got to put your name first.'

'Gabe.'

'I know.' I keyed his name into my contacts.

Because he was a friend of Jane's husband, Charles, I felt safe with him. When I met him for a drink he didn't stare at the bartender's cleavage. His hands looked weathered and his head was mostly bald and shiny; I wondered whether the hair loss bothered him.

'I've just moved out to the country and given up my allotment. I love growing vegetables. My new place has at least two acres, but it's like a field.'

'I don't know how big an acre is.'

'A football pitch is about one and a half acres.'

'That's massive. Are you using a rotavator?'

'No, because it doesn't get rid of the roots. I'm doing it a bit at a time, with a spade.'

He was *perfect*: a gardener with a hands-on approach.

We met for a picnic. Lying under a tree, we chatted and laughed. We went for a walk round a pond where we saw two frogs mating in the grass. We kissed and the world turned Disney so that I felt like a child again except I had a hot liquid feeling, not in the pit of my stomach as it so often says in best-selling novels but much lower down. A spring welled up in me, as green, deep and neglected as the pond.

After I'd known Gabe about a month, I cooked him a meal and he ended up staying over. I didn't mind him seeing my blobby bits, my jelly belly or my orange-peel skin because he had a belly too.

'And my eyebrows have gone bristly, and I have to trim my nose hair,' he said.

He smelled like soil after rain.

He didn't dig me up. No pits, ditches or trenches, which was all for the best because who wants a fork or spade stuck in them, let alone a pickaxe? What he did was hollow out fallen tree trunks to create a system of conduits that carried water from my new well to wherever I needed it. He cleaned the algae from my spring till it ran clear, while I had fun working his old-fashioned pump handle up and down. I loved the sensation of cool water flowing over my skin. It didn't matter if I looked wrinkled or flabby when I felt so good. I loved the sparkle of sunshine on the stream. I never felt lonely, even when Gabe wasn't there.

I began to cultivate splashes of blue cornflowers, yellow dahlias and green hellebore that flowered all winter. I grew vegetables and fruit: at first only spinach and potatoes, but then, the following summer, I tried courgettes in pots, sugar-snap peas and pumpkins. Getting carried away, I planted and harvested watermelons, artichokes and fennel. At work more women requested makeovers and bought products, so I earned more commission.

'You look great. Anybody would think you'd saved up and had a face-lift,' said Kitty as she picked a juicy strawberry from a bed.

My kids were happy because I didn't nag them to visit. My cooking improved when I could add home-grown onions and carrots to my casseroles. I no longer had to eat the same dish four days running because Gabe, with an appetite sharpened by his irrigation work, consumed half at one sitting; he praised my cooking.

'He's *perfect*,' said Jane.

'You've finally learned some sense,' said Lizzie.

Reader, I married him. He began to expect regular meals, take control of the TV remote and leave the toilet seat up. My garden is flourishing, but sometimes I wonder whether I was too influenced by my sisters.

THE NEMESIS OF MERYTON

Clare Girvan

Miss Mary Bennet was quietly reading in the window overlooking the garden when she became aware that her mother had entered the room and was regarding her with some irritation.

'I declare, Mary, you will drive me distracted with your reading and your needlework,' she complained. 'All your sisters have made advantageous matches, yet here you still sit as if husbands are going to come knocking at our door. I beg you to change your mind about the ball.'

'I have no wish to attend a ball to get a husband, Mamma,' said Miss Bennet, setting down her copy of *The Mysteries of Udolpho*. 'But I own I might welcome some small diversion. Life is so much less exciting than in books.' She sighed. 'I shall go into Meryton and purchase some more sewing needles.'

Meryton that day proved chilly and dull, and furnished her with no one of her acquaintance to converse with, so she made her purchases with scant enthusiasm and prepared to return to Longbourn. But on leaving Mrs Hazelwood's haberdashery, her attention was distracted by a loud report and a commotion further up the street, where a small crowd was gathering. Reverend Forbes was already at the scene, kneeling by an inert female figure.

'Who is it?' asked Miss Bennet.

'It is your namesake,' said the reverend gentleman. 'Miss Mary Bennett from the post office.'

'Miss Mary—? Is she—?' Miss Bennet ventured.

'I do not understand,' said Reverend Forbes. 'I have known her all her life and she has not an enemy in the world.'

More shots sounded a little way off and a man of military bearing was observed to fall to the ground, bleeding profusely. His assailant ran back to Miss Bennet, carrying a smoking firearm and exclaiming harshly, 'If you wish to live, come with me. The Nemesis will be upon you in a few minutes. I have a carriage waiting.'

'Sir,' protested Miss Bennet. 'I have no intention— '

He seized her by the hand and hustled her down the street and into a carriage and drove furiously away. Miss Bennet attempted to unfasten the door, but it was secure. She fell back against the cushions in despair.

Once clear of habitation, he reined in the horses and turned to her.

'Be assured, madam,' he said, 'I have no wish to hurt you. On the contrary, I am here to be of assistance. My name is Warrant Officer Sergeant Willoughby, DF84486. We shall be safe here for a while,' he continued, 'but it is my melancholy duty to inform you that you have been assigned for termination.'

Miss Bennet stared at him.

'Termination, sir? You mean I am – to die?' Sergeant Willoughby nodded tersely. 'But why?' she whispered. 'I have done nothing.'

'No, madam, you have not. But you will. I cannot stress too strongly how vital it is that you should live.'

'The gentleman with whom you quarrelled just now…?' said Miss Bennet. 'How was he able to rise after such severe injuries?'

'He is no man, madam, but an automaton. A machine. A Nemesis, Ironclad, Model 5.'

'A machine?' stammered Miss Bennet. 'But he was bleeding…'

'Such automata are difficult to detect,' said Willoughby. 'They have hair, skin, flesh and blood, like a man, but beneath are driven by clockwork and several small steam engines. The invention of a Mr Babbage forty years hence.'

'I cannot understand you, sir,' said Miss Bennet. 'It is not possible to construct such a creature.'

'You are right,' said the sergeant. 'At the present time, it is not possible, but in the future, such beings will be commonplace.'

'You are telling me that this – creature – is from the future? You are mocking me.'

'A possible future only,' said Willoughby.

'And you are from the future too?'

'I am.'

'I see,' said Miss Bennet, and again attempted to open the carriage door. Willoughby caught her arm and Miss Bennet instantly sank her teeth into his hand.

Willoughby's grip did not slacken.

'An automaton does not feel pain,' he said, coldly. 'I do. I must ask you to refrain from injuring me in future.'

'Please,' said Miss Bennet. 'I beg you to let me go.'

'You must heed me,' said Willoughby. 'The automaton is inhuman. It has no sense of pity, remorse or fear, and it cannot be reasoned or bargained with. It will not cease in its endeavour until you are no more.'

'But why does it wish to – kill me?'

'There was a war, that is to say, there will be a war, forty years from now. A dreadful war against unknown invaders, in which everything was destroyed and the world run by automata.' Miss Bennet gasped. 'There were survivors, residing in the ruins. We starved, attempting to hide from the Gatherers. They would apprehend us and remove us to camps, where we were kept alive for labour. Day and night, we must needs load corpses for disposal. Many died. The rest of us were brought to the edge of extinction.' He paused. 'But a saviour was amongst us. He taught us resistance and how to conquer the automata. He lives still. His name is Orlando Bennet.' He paused again, gazing fixedly at her.

'Orlando Bennet? Can you mean he is a relation of mine?'

'More than that, madam. He is your son. Your unborn son.'

Miss Bennet stared at him, dumbfounded.

'You are mistaken, sir. I have no husband.'

'Nevertheless, it is true. And he it is who led his people in the fight against the automata, in order to save the world.'

Miss Bennet shivered.

'Are you cold, madam?'

'A little.'

Willoughby reached into the back of the carriage. 'Might I suggest that we share this blanket? I mean no impertinence, but it is our sole means of remaining warm.'

Miss Bennet subdued her reservations and gratefully accepted the consolation of the blanket and the warmth engendered by the sergeant.

'Have you a first name, sir?' she enquired, tentatively.

'Gideon. May I have the honour to use your own?'

'You may. If you truly have come through time – tell me, how does it feel?'

'It is not pleasant. I experienced a sensation that must somewhat

153

resemble being born…of being torn out of something, and found myself in an alleyway.'

'And how are you to get back?'

'I cannot. We have no means of facilitating such a return.' He shifted uncomfortably. 'I believe I have a slight injury, Mary.'Miss Bennet drew back Willoughby's coat and recoiled at the sight of his ensanguined shirt front.

'Good God, it is blood!'

'It is of no consequence.'

'But we must find a surgeon…'

'That is unlikely in so remote a spot.'

'Then you must let me attend to it,' she said.

She took a handkerchief from her pocket and attempted to clean the wound.

'Gideon – would you tell me about – my son? Is he a good man?'

'He is in all things the most admirable. There are those who would sacrifice their lives should he require it. I am of their number.'

'And…might I enquire as to his father? I know of no one…'

'He spoke little of him.'

'Did – my son – order you to come here?'

'No. I came of my own volition. I wished above all else to make the acquaintance of the legend.'

'The legend?'

'Miss Mary Bennet, who instructed her son in the art of warfare, and instigated the revolution… it was an honour that I sought with all the vigour at my command.'

'But I protest the profoundest ignorance of all things military,' exclaimed Miss Bennet, 'and I have never so much as quitted the confines of Meryton… '

'Experience and necessity will bestow proficiency upon you. I have a message from your son, which I have committed to memory, lest it fell into the wrong hands.'

She passed a hand across her brow. 'From – him? To me?'

'My dear Mother,' Willoughby began. 'It is with profound gratitude for your courage in the dark time to come that I send these words. In order to do this, it is imperative that you be strong beyond your imagining. If you do not survive, I shall not exist and the world will come to an end. Your affectionate son, Orlando.'

'I understand,' said Miss Bennet. 'This automaton is to kill me in order that my son shall not be born, is that not so?'

'That is indubitably the case. He has already killed three ladies called Mary Bennett, evidently by means of the Fashionable List. You have been fortunate.'

'I should hardly say that. Can you not stop it?'

'I shall endeavour to do so. The Nemesis is able to track its quarry over great distances, so it is expedient that we go forward with all despatch. But first we need rest and a refuge.'

The room at the modest inn was small but adequate, and Willoughby began to unpack a bag.

'I trust you are not averse to explosives?' he asked as she stared at the items extracted therefrom, which included some metal tubes and a large tin of black powder.

'I have no experience of them,' she said. 'But it is doubtless incumbent upon me to learn. Show me what I must do.'

'The Nemesis is armed with an automatic carbine, as am I,' he said. 'But if I can construct some Congreve Rockets, we may prevail. They are somewhat antiquated, but effective.'

'Then we must set to work directly,' said Miss Bennet, rolling up her sleeves.

She proved an apt pupil and presently four rockets lay on the table. He unexpectedly took her hand and drew her to him.

'It saddens me,' he said, 'to see your beautiful earth and know that soon it may be no more. All will be gone.'

'All?' she said. A tear fell down her cheek.

'You need rest,' he said. 'Lie down and I will complete the remainder.'

She obeyed and made no demur when presently he lay beside her.

'You have no objection?'

'None whatsoever.'

The sun was scarcely above the horizon when they arose, thoroughly refreshed. Miss Bennet observed that Willoughby had been abroad before her, and had already kicked away the carriage window and strapped six completed rockets in the back.

'He will have gained on us somewhat,' he said. 'But horses must rest, if he himself does not.'

'The more reason to start at once,' said Miss Bennet. 'Have you recovered from your wound?'

'I am well enough,' he responded.

Willoughby whipped up the horses and they drove in silence for some way, but presently he turned to her, grim-faced.

'He is behind us,' he said. 'Take the reins.'

Miss Bennet did so with determination, while Willoughby scrambled to the rockets. The automaton was gaining on them, unhampered by the weight of a carriage. Willoughby fired the first rocket, which exploded ahead of their pursuer. He muttered an oath and fired a second. The Nemesis responded with a shot from his carbine, which hit Willoughby on the shoulder, disabling it. With his good arm Willoughby fired two more rockets, unseating the Nemesis from his horse onto the road, where he lay still.

'He is not dead,' said Willoughby. 'We must find a place of safety.'

'I think I can see a building in the wood,' suggested Miss Bennet.

Concealing the carriage in a grove of trees, Willoughby appropriated the remaining rockets and they hastened through undergrowth towards the sound of rushing water, where stood a locked wooden edifice. The sergeant gave the door an energetic kick and they found themselves in a sawmill containing tree trunks, planks of wood and much sawdust. To the side of the mill a vast, motionless wheel was partially submerged in the water and presently held in check by a lever.

'Will he find us?' whispered Miss Bennet.

'He will,' he responded. 'But we have the advantage of surprise.' He began setting up the rockets to face the door.

Miss Bennet seized a piece of wood and swung it through the air.

'O, I shall give him such a surprise,' she said doughtily.

For the first time in their acquaintance, Willoughby laughed.

'Have a care, Mary,' he said. 'Our opponent is not so easy to destroy.'

'I hear hoof beats,' she said. 'He is here.'

Through the window, they observed the Nemesis dismount and approach the mill, carbine at the ready. The Nemesis caught sight of the lever and advanced it to its full capacity, whereupon the great wheel began to turn as the water filled it, gathering momentum. Inside, the building vibrated alarmingly as huge wooden cogs engaged and linked together and the vertical saw commenced its jolting progress along the empty workbench.

'He means to confuse us,' said Willoughby. 'Keep a clear head, and stay away from the machinery.'

The figure of the Nemesis appeared in the doorway and Willoughby fired the first of the rockets. It struck him directly and he fell in flames, setting light to some wood splinters. Willoughby fired another rocket. The Nemesis got to his feet, his clothes and skin hanging in smoking tatters, revealing part of the engines beneath, but still he came on, firing a shot which brought Willoughby to his knees. He shot again, but was abruptly knocked off his feet by a violent blow from the piece of wood wielded by Miss Bennet which sent him crashing into the mechanism of the saw.

They watched, with mingled horror and relief, as the automaton went down with an awesome screeching cry, crushed by the great wheels, its skeletal arms flailing helplessly. Particles of metal flew about the room, amid clouds of steam and sawdust, offering danger to life and limb, but when all was over, the last remains of the Nemesis were finally still.

'He is gone!' shouted Miss Bennet jubilantly, but her satisfaction was short-lived. Willoughby was lying on the ground with scarcely a breath of life left in him. Weeping, she bent over him.

'Gideon, you must live,' she urged him. 'I cannot complete the mission alone.'

His eyes opened and he gave a weak smile.

'My Mary will know what to do,' he said.

*

Mary Bennet and her mother were sitting in the sunny garden. Mary was wearing a lace shawl which adequately concealed her condition.

'I believe the regiment may visit soon,' said Mrs Bennet.

'Do not think of it, Mamma. You know I can never marry now, and I cannot raise my son here. I have work to do.'

'Yes, my dear, so you say, but I wish you will not leave, even though it is best under the circumstances. I think we should go indoors now. From the look of the sky, there is a storm coming.'

'Yes, Mamma,' rejoined Miss Bennet. 'I know.'

MONEY THE HARD WAY

L E Yates

Eugene had been annoying her all morning so when he pointed out the sign for Huntsville Prison Rodeo she kept her head turned away and pretended to be admiring a field of sorghum. 'You have a strange idea of fun,' was all she contented herself with saying, as she stepped out of the car, but she knew the disgust in her voice was enough. His friend, Boulanger, and Sissy, Boulanger's limp fiancée, both stopped smirking.

Eugene scowled. 'Oh, come on, Lydia, if you worked in your father's stuffy bank all day you'd think this was a hoot.'

'I just think you've got a strange idea of fun, that's all.' The scruffy lot edged with weeds and empty soda cans reminded her of the poor side of town in Corpus Christi, where she'd lived with her first husband, George.

'Do you girls want a coke before we go in?' Eugene flashed his wallet in the direction of a thin black man buckling under the weight of a tray laden with drinks and chips of ice. Lydia tilted the brim of her hat forward and wondered how long the man had been standing out in the dazzling heat. Since her first marriage had ended this was the kind of thought she found herself having more often.

'Hey, Eugene, I've got this.' Boulanger tugged his wallet out of his duck trousers. 'Don't want to bankrupt the Bryant Mutual.'

'Relax, Boulanger, it's on me.'

Lydia let the men tussle while she stared off at the families pouring out of rusty pick-ups and flocking into the arena. She wasn't thirsty and didn't give two hoots who paid. Really, Eugene could be such a bore. His good looks – crinkly, blonde hair and a long, sensitive face – only made his tediousness more pronounced. When she turned back, surprised they hadn't yet moved on, Eugene had his friend in a headlock. Boulanger's lanky arms flailed as their scuffling feet raised plumes of dust.

'Boys will be boys,' Sissy simpered at her.

'Apparently so.' Lydia had no doubt, even as she spoke, that this would be noted down as another instance of her wickedly sharp tongue and relayed to an eager gathering at church tomorrow. The scuffle ended abruptly. Boulanger seemed to have won, at least, he gave a mock-bow as he presented her with an ice-cold bottle.

She lagged behind the group as they headed towards the arena but

161

Eugene dropped his pace. 'Hey, what do you say, we could have a double wedding with Boulanger and Sissy? They've already set a date for August.'

'I'd rather eat my own head than get married at the same time as Sissy Chandler.'

'Where do you pick up such expressions?' Eugene gave a fond shake of his head which made her want to punch him in the eye.

'That yellow hat with the daisies! She's got no taste at all. Just thinking about her in that dress makes me want to scream.'

'Well, it's true she's not as pretty as you.' He smirked, but this wasn't the response she'd been looking for.

When they finally got inside, the shade was a blessed relief. The voice over the tannoy was coy between the crackling. 'Never mind, folks, he's going to be plenty good with all the practice he'll get. He's eligible for ninety-seven more of these affairs.'

The fatty stench of butter popcorn on the humid air made Lydia want to be sick. 'Blow chunks' – that's what George used to say, a foul expression. He'd say things like that deliberately then look at her with a sly expression on his face. This teasing was part of what made him so infuriating, so attractive. A chestnut mustang shot out of the chute, the rider's zebra-striped shirt a blur. For a few seconds the man seemed glued on, one hand waving bravely in the air, before he crumpled to the side and was bounced off. The crowd whooped.

'Aaaaand that concludes the Prison Rodeo's Bucking Broncs. Let's give those riders a nice big hand.'

Sissy was pouring over the listings with Boulanger. 'Say, who do you fancy for the next event?'

Lydia could feel Eugene fidgeting next to her but she didn't bother to check her programme. She didn't care who was up next, was only glad when the whining blue-grass fiddle faded away and the prison band trooped out of the arena.

'Are you ready, folks?' the tannoy blared. 'This next one's a lil' ole game called Money the Hard Way and I've just been told that for whichever intrepid adventurer snatches the purse from the bull's horns there's a whopping two hundred dollars inside.'

'You're not watching, Lyd.' Eugene dug her in the side with his elbow.

Lydia wasn't. She was thinking how at twenty-one all her girlfriends were taking their first hopeful steps into marriage and there she was with one failure already behind her. Her mother never tired of reminding her she'd been lucky to catch Eugene's attention.

'Look now, here they go!' Eugene dug her in the ribs again, a gesture that probably passed for good humour among his fraternity buddies. Lydia turned her eyes scornfully towards the sawdust oval. The convicts filed out and stood in loose groups, some tucking in their shirts, some tugging nervously at the crotch of their pants. There was something so familiar about one man at the end of the row that her heart stopped for a second but no sooner had the jolt of recognition passed through her than she'd dismissed it. Ridiculous, it couldn't possibly be. Eugene and the wedding and stupid Sissy were making her over-wrought, that was all, but she peered at the man despite herself. The second glance was enough for her to be sure.

Despite the baggy black and white uniform Lydia could see George hadn't lost his powerful build. He looked at ease with his striped shirt rolled up over lean biceps. It only surprised her a little that she wasn't at all surprised to see him there. A greasy hank of black hair fell from under his wide-brimmed cowboy hat. She scoured his shadowed face. The more she could remember the more she could hate him and that smiling, lanky red-haired friend of his. His skin seemed a little more crinkled around his narrow eyes but his mouth was still as wide as a frog's. He clapped a man with a child's chubby face on the back, and flashed him an easy smile which seemed to reach all the way to the back of the stands. Carefully she added this new version of his face to the past ones she had filed away.

'Saw two men get killed on this one last year,' the fat man next to Eugene boasted. His jowls drooped like a bloodhound's and he wore a tie like a string of wet liquorice. Lydia felt him glance over to see if he had impressed her. She kept her eyes fixed on the arena but her pulse quickened. George could be killed and she could watch it happen.

163

Her ex-husband stood now, one hand on his hip, head cocked as if this were no more deadly than idling outside the county store. As Lydia stared he dipped his head and let out a long plume of brown tobacco juice. His head was still down when the chute opened with a clank and the bull charged into the arena.

Men tumbled like skittles, one tossed then another in quick succession. A hat drifted to the ground. The bull stood over one fallen man, contemplative for a moment before it lowered its head and tried to spike him but he scrambled to his feet and staggered away. A wiry Mexican darted in from the side and mis-timed a grab at the purse before retreating. The announcer's voice spooled on but it had no place in her thoughts. She lost sight of George as the men whirled. Where was he? There. She let out a low cry of excitement and grabbed Eugene's hand as the bull charged again.

'Now you're getting into it, Lyd,' crowed Eugene. 'I knew you would.'

'Don't you worry, Lydia, them guys is plenty fast,' said Boulanger.

She caught sight of George in a loose knot of prisoners but, as the bull lowered its head and trampled over a man it'd already felled, Lydia watched him peel away from the safety of the group, moving with a familiar athletic grace. He was faster than anyone else but he was still only halfway down the bull's huge flank when it kicked its hind-legs in the air and bucked its head towards him. George swerved, dipped under a horn which flashed in his face, and reached out a hand. Lydia squeezed Eugene's knuckles. George seemed frozen in this pose as time stretched, then his hand closed over the purse hanging between the bull's eyes. But the next moment he was flying through the air, legs over his head like he was climbing an upside down staircase. He hit the ground hard. Lydia couldn't hear anything at that moment, not the announcer, nor the crowd, nor the clank and bellow of the other cattle in the pen.

The bull charged off joyously, flipping two other men over, leaving George crumpled where he'd fallen. He lay on his back on the sawdust and didn't move. Cold water flowed over Lydia as she watched a stretcher team in white amble out from under the stands.

A crowd of prisoners blocked her view of his head. She could see only his broad chest. His chest. His beautiful chest. She saw George lying on his back on the timber deck of the house on Ocean Drive, his suntan-oiled torso dense with muscle and dusted with black hair, a cigarette crooked out of his mouth, eyes closed, t-shirt pillowed under his head. He hadn't moved as she'd hove into sight carrying two bottles of beer. She'd thought he was asleep until he lifted his head and winked at her.

She waited.

'Would you look at that!' Boulanger wolf-whistled as Sissy clutched his arm. The crowd roared. Lydia lifted her gaze dumbly. A flat-footed white man with a paunch wobbling in front of him had taken advantage of the bull's distraction to run across and snatch the purse.

'Son of a bitch, he's done it!' hollered Eugene's neighbour. His friend elbowed him. 'Sorry, ma'am.' He swept off his hat to Lydia.

Lydia turned her head away from the ring as nausea swelled inside her. When she looked back the stretcher team had reached George. A bucket of water splashed in his face but still he lay there.

Lydia dropped Eugene's hand and stood up.

'Lyd, you okay?'

She pushed past him.

'What the heck?'

The fat man in the string-tie and his friend half-stood to let her leave.

'Where the hell are you going?' Eugene called.

She fought her way out through the crowds, past a Rodeo Clown and a churchy-looking couple who muttered, 'Well, I never,' as she shoved past them. Outside, the air was wet. She stumbled across the cinder parking lot. By the time she'd found Eugene's car, he'd caught up with her.

'What in hell's wrong with you, Lydia, running off like that?'

'I feel... I felt sick. Just take me home please. I don't want to fight with you, Eugene.'

He raged. She'd ruined his day, his only day off a week. What would Boulanger and Sissy think? What was he supposed to tell them? In the end she'd let herself cry so he'd agree to take her home.

Her hands shook as Eugene turned the key and pulled out of the lot. They drove through the brown, empty fields, her thoughts whirling, but as she neared home she didn't see George's still figure lying on the sawdust, but instead the gleeful face of the flat-footed man as he'd snatched the bag of money from between the bull's horns. She took a handkerchief from her bag, dabbed her eyes dry and repaired her make-up as best she could. By the time Eugene had pulled into her parent's drive and let the engine die with an angry cough, she was composed enough to turn a dazzling smile on him. She'd already decided she wouldn't cry any more, at least, not in public.

THE GREY LADY

Susan Piper

Who do you think I am?

I know your heartbeat quickens at the glimpse you have caught of me in the corner of your eye. I am impossible. I am the one you will later whisper to friends about having seen. Or perhaps, after a few tongue-loosening cups at the Greyfriar, you will rant boastfully, swearing on someone's grave that you have seen me. You will wonder over whether I am the shade of a jilted lady, a governess, an unhappy servant or maybe even the writer herself. Strike out that last thought! She has achieved enough influence without your belief in her ghost.

But who am I?

Turn your head slowly and look me full in the face. Trust me – you have no reason to be afraid for I am totally without power to harm or help. I will try to stay still and not tremble out of focus. Perhaps if I move in front of the window? No. Now I am washed out by the present day light. In front of this dark cabinet, stained by generations of finger tips and regular oiling? No. I absorb the darkness and dim to invisibility.

Dear reader, prove the 'dear' by focussing long and hard. I believe your attention could give me a little substance. Let me reveal myself to you. If you have read the great writer's books, you might recognise me. But will you be disappointed? Why not the more memorable character? Why not my sister? Why not the one who replaced me in our creator's affections? Strong, solid, proud Elizabeth; what need has she of your belief?

I beg you – for I have no pride – to put aside your prejudice. Let me relate how I came to these reduced circumstances and let your understanding fill in the shadow that is all you can see of me from the corner of your eye. She gave me her name but that was before I shamed her.

The Assemblies were hot and stuffy, especially the room reserved for dancing, which pleased the girls' mother for it brought a fetching rose to the cheeks of the two daughters she watched so diligently, ensuring her position afforded her a direct line of sight with each of them at all times.

To Elizabeth, her oldest but one, the heat of the room added the mischievous sparkle that had earned affection of friends and family and the dedicated mother made a note to herself to speak to Lizzie about not appearing over-familiar.

But for Jane, her eldest, the blossom in her cheeks completed the radiance that isolated her from the rest of the company; the glow that set her apart in her own pool of soft-edged elegance. Jane sat with her back straight, poised but without a hint of haughtiness and the mother congratulated herself on having produced at least one daughter who could use every gesture, every nuance of her sweet, low-pitched voice to gain and hold control over any room.

But the mother had other responsibilities that evening and while she kept the corridor of supervision open with the older two, she was now and then necessarily distracted. Her over-excited younger daughters could not be relied on to comport themselves with anything like decorum. There was also the spying out of eligible bachelors to manage; particularly their new neighbour, the handsome, young and well-heeled Mr Bingley. And while her mother was distracted by the weight of her many responsibilities, Jane proved that she could use her charms most effectively.

But it was not the targeted Mr Bingley who received Jane's skill and attention. The other, a friend in Mr Bingley's party, had drawn her eye from the moment he arrived, walking comfortably in the middle of his own circle of solitude. When she felt his eye light on her soon after, the rest of the room fogged and slowed; only the two of them remained animated. Before long their circles overlapped. At the stranger's insistence, Mr Bingley provided an introduction. It did not take long for Jane to let him lead her onto the floor. Through every step, even at opposite ends of the line, she felt this Mr Darcy's gaze and each brush of their gloved fingertips became almost an impropriety.

When Jane's mother saw the line her daughter cast was successfully ensnaring Mr Darcy she bustled to Lizzie's side, warning her that she must not let Mr Bingley escape. What a triumph it would be if she could safely ensure two daughters' futures in a single night! Even if it meant several days of sick headaches, plain broth and cake to recover from the exertion, it would be half her life's work complete – in a matter of hours. For the briefest moment, she relaxed her guard and went in search of a cooling ice.

Jane, too, left the busyness of the ballroom to refresh herself, knowing full well that she pulled Mr Darcy mercilessly after her.

In a shadowy alcove, public enough for decency but private enough for honesty, he won her first name, he won the promise of a meeting the next day and he dropped a kiss into her gloved palm. He left her there and, out of sight of all, she leant her forehead against the cool glass of the window to work against the warmth spread from the kissed place until even the flimsy stuff of her best gown suffocated and constricted.

In the night following the ball, Jane moved to the furthest edge of the bed she shared with Lizzie and waited until her sister's easiness of conscience took her into sleep. Then Jane let fantasy pull the glove from Darcy's hand. She traced each faint, dark hair on each long finger. She kissed that hand so thoroughly that she moved onto the other and then she placed those hands where she hoped they would ease the restless beat of her blood in her ears and still her rapid breath.

After writing this, the other Jane, also spent a sleepless night. She had not intended this passion, not foreseen how intensely her own sensibilities would catch fire in the wake of mine. She had designed Darcy for Lizzie! I was to have been the light to Lizzie's dark cleverness; I was to have been the beauty suffering in silence while Lizzie gave rein to righteous anger. This attraction between Darcy and me was outside the writer's carefully constructed plot.

Her feverish struggle as my passion aroused extreme sensations in her own breast was doubled by her betrayal by me – her creature! Added to this, she knew she could never share this story with anyone; not if she wanted her own name attached to it. Earning recognition and admiration for her skill, was always a driving force behind her pen.

And so, while I lay in my bed thinking only of him, she plotted her re-writes.

The next day, Mrs Bennet's first daughter chose her outfit with care. The morning passed slowly, with frequent trips to her room to make subtle changes to her appearance. She returned to the mirror again and again, trying to imagine how his eyes would read her hair, her face and her figure. As she rehearsed casual words that would allow her to escape her family and walk to the secluded place that held such promise, her heart stuttered and she breathed deeply, willing away the blush that rose from her throat to her cheekbones.

When her sisters tried to draw her into a game or a walk, she silenced them with the look that only her family had ever felt the force of. 'Jane's in one of her moods,' complained Lydia when she failed to engage her sister in another round of reviewing the excitement of the previous evening. Even Lizzie withdrew, hurt, when Jane pointed out that they spent every waking hour together and if there was nothing new to add to their conversation, Jane would rather do without it just now.

It was at the moment that she went to search for her coat to leave the house that Lydia's shriek cut the air. 'There's two of them! It's both of them!' The younger sister ran giggling as she rounded up her sisters to peer through the gauze curtains of the morning room.

Courtesies having being exchanged, it was Mr Bingley who suggested a walk and skirting past Lizzie and Darcy, held the door for Jane who had been hovering there, ready to make her escape.

Jane took every opportunity as the two pairs walked in the encouraging sunshine to get a little apart from the group, sometimes hurrying forward, other times dawdling to examine some leaf or other, giving Mr Darcy opportunity to move to her side. She grew more and more frustrated as the man continued to listen attentively to Lizzie's lively tales of village life while Mr Bingley, ever the gentleman, rushed to Jane's side to keep her included in the group. When he took her hand to help her over a treacherous place in the path, she drew away from his touch as soon as politeness permitted. She stifled a yawn as he spoke at length of his pleasure in and plans for his new home in this neighbourhood and she hardly heard when he exclaimed, almost dewy-eyed, that he had never hoped to find such congenial company out of town, beaming into her face with an open smile. Her lack of attention unsettled him and he finally remained quiet, tugging nervously at the wrist of one glove or the other.

Over the coming days Jane watched Darcy's regard for Lizzie grow. He had found her 'quite pretty' at the ball where they met but now noticed that her eyes filled her otherwise fairly unremarkable features with an intelligence that he could not remember finding in any other member of his female acquaintance. Lizzie, confident in her knowledge of the masculine race, had stated more than once that if a man liked a woman, that woman must surely be an idiot if she did not realise it. But she did not pick up the slightest hint of his changed opinion. And Jane, for all her efforts, could not reverse that change.

Before I could even make the promised meeting, she reduced me. She stole my childhood of healthy arguments and lively games with my sisters and made me retiring. She took the light that filled our father's eye whenever I entered the room and turned it towards Lizzie, leaving me his kind compliments but denying me his pride and his confidence.

I begged her, first respectfully and then with tears. Over and over, she tried to calm my desire for him; to douse the heat that enveloped her whenever her pen brought us together. I had behaved badly and she couldn't forgive me. Finally, she tore up page after page of my passion – my life – and with a deep frown above a relieved smile, placed each piece on the fire.

When the two sisters met as Mrs Bingley and Mrs Darcy, meetings that grew rarer as Lizzie spent less and less time in town, Lizzie would ask Jane why she never stopped her husband when he repeated a story for the hundredth time. Sometimes she suggested that Jane could afford to miss part of a season in town with the same relentless throng of the same people, doing the same things; she could leave the endless social organising and come and stay with her sister in Derbyshire.

An exemplary wife, Jane always answered, 'Dear Lizzie, my husband is the best of men and I will be what he needs me to be.'

I was given my happy ending. Sweet Bingley became even less solid than I. I remember the day he finally dissolved. His full, handsome side whiskers tickled my cheek as he planted a brotherly kiss. 'Goodbye dear heart. My good girl.' But there was no real sorrow in his voice. He was just gone.

And I faded. I have not even been left with one jealous bone that would let

173

me resent Lizzie's happiness. I have no anger, no bitterness, no hope except for your ability to make me a bit more substantial.

A drifting shape, I walk the galleries and staircases where I was conceived, buffeted by the breeze of inattention. The most response I can hope for is a gentle smile of recognition but more often I perceive a shiver of unease. She has not even given me the substance to startle! I hold out my hands – I want to claw at the attention of the living, scratch them into a reaction as I used to tug Lizzie's hair when we were little girls. But it can only be her – that author – who can put feeling flesh on these porcelain bones. And she is gone. She didn't even leave me the ability to hate her. Hate? Not gentle Jane who under the writer's relentless editing became the one who saw the good in everyone.

Dear reader, when you read the book of our lives, think of me. I don't mean pityingly or empathetically – just think of me. And please don't be distracted by other characters or writerly cleverness. And please don't think I totally blame my writer; her renown even all these years later proves that her decisions must have been sound ones. You, dear reader, you have a responsibility to fill in the empty places.

The young man, just up from the country could not take his eyes off his hostess. He had been advised to accept every invitation he received from the Bingleys. The fame of Mrs Bingley's grace and the generosity of her hospitality had not done justice to the reality. She made every guest feel that their comfort was her personal crusade. Standing in an alcove public enough for propriety but private enough for honesty, she had laid her hand on his cheek, telling him that he was always welcome in her home and she hoped he would look on her as a friend. Before he could respond to her words or to the something that lay behind them, she was gone, as silently and serenely as a phantom.

So when you get a glimmer of me in the corner of your eye, when you shiver because I walk through you as dusk stirs everything into shadow, think of me. Think of me powerfully enough to stroke my hair, warm my cold fingers. I won't be any trouble. I thank you for your kindness.

That is all I am allowed to say.

THE POWER OF NURSE ROOKE

Anne Thomas

A servant's life is not without its pleasures, but one has to have a keen sense of humour to see beyond the drudgery and loss of freedom. To be at another's beck and call is wearing for one of my temperament, so it was no grief to me when Mr and Mrs Smallbone decided to return to their native Scotland, where (Mrs S assured me) the air was more healthy than that of England. Nurse Rooke's services would no longer be required. I collected the money owed me and sat down to write to my sister.

The next day, I stood with the other servants to wave Mr and Mrs Smallbone off and then climbed the steep stairs to my room for the last time. I had a ticket for the afternoon mail to Bath where my sister awaited me. Emily always kept a room ready for me in Westgate Buildings, where I might stay whilst I looked for work. I can turn my hand to most things, but experience has made me skilled with the sick, so a little private nursing would fill the gap.

I loved the road to Bath, no matter how uncomfortable the journey. It was always busy and full of conveyances of every type. It was not unusual to come across a collision between a carter and a young rake – the road was full of them – high-spirited and reckless young men, showing off inadequate skills and driving overheated horses. All too frequently they were the worse for their stop at the last hostelry, too drunk to be sensible to danger. In times past, I had occasionally earned a half-sovereign by climbing down and mending cracked heads. After the long confinement of the servants' quarters in Portsmouth, I was eager for life in all its variety and would have welcomed the distraction. We encountered curricles and carts aplenty along the way, and one near collision which almost cost us a wheel ('Look out, Elliot,' his passenger had cried, 'You'll have us all in the ditch!'). However, my nursing skills were not required and I arrived in Bath at last, no richer than when I set out on my journey.

My sister had sent William, a gawky lad of fifteen or sixteen, with few wits and less grace, to meet me and carry my bags. I was glad of his help and followed him the short distance to Westgate Buildings. I pressed two pence into his none-too-clean hand and he sidled off, testing the coins between ill-favoured teeth and leaving me to carry the bags in, myself.

'Clemmie,' Emily wiped her hands on her apron and greeted me with a sisterly kiss. 'It is good to see you.'

'Emily,' I returned the kiss. 'You look very well – but very tired. I have come not a moment too soon.'

'I will not argue with that. We are very busy just now, with the season under way. But come and sit by the fire. A cup of tea will revive us both.'

I removed my hat and I joined Emily by the fire. I was weary, and glad of the warmth.

'Who have you in mind for me, sister?' I asked, as soon as the preliminaries were done and our mutual health assured.

'There's a Major Richards and his mouse of a wife in the front rooms,' she began, and then went on to list four or five more potential clients. She saved the best for last.

'Lady Dalrymple and her daughter, Miss Carteret – of Laura Place – have inquired for a nurse. Miss Carteret is unwell and Lady Dalrymple has heard of your skill.'

'And how did she hear of that, sister dear?'

'It cost only a half crown to the head footman – less would have been an impertinence!'

'How does she ail, this daughter?'

'Miss Carteret is sadly indisposed – she is afflicted by being her mother's daughter!' Emily burst out laughing and, tired as I was, I shared the joke.

'Too much mother and not enough beaux?' I gasped, as my breath returned.

'She's as plain as a pike staff and has only her rank to support her.'

'Well, in Bath that should pass unnoticed, if she can carry a smart gown,' I returned. 'I'll go along to see her in the morning.'

'If you are not too tired, sister, would you mind seeing one lady tonight? I took her in out of kindness. She was very ill when she arrived and, knowing that you would soon be home, I thought: "Clementine will help here." You will, will you not, sister?'

178

I sighed. I had risen before dawn the day before and worked until nearly noon. I had been on the road ever since and I longed for my bed.

'Of course,' I heard myself reply. 'Where is she?'

Mrs Smith was clearly in great pain. I had seldom seen a woman of her young age, so crippled with rheumatism. I made her as comfortable as I could and promised to return first thing in the morning.

'You will not bleed me, will you?' she asked, eyes wide with fear.

'No, of course not,' I assured her.

As I found my bed, I blessed my sister. Her astute mind had kept us both from want ever since our father had died leaving us with little to live on. All hopes of marriage had been dashed when the French war took away our young men. So many had perished on foreign soil; so many, like us, lived on, settling for 'second best'.

Over the next few days Mrs Smith improved a little. Sleep came to her, refreshing spirits long-tested by sickness and pain. But there was something more, something which troubled her and shadowed her face when she believed herself to be unobserved. Once, in her sleep, she cried out: 'Mr Elliot, have pity!' and I wondered what it meant. Give her time, I thought, she will speak when she is ready.

In the meantime I busied myself with the other patients my sister had found, and made myself pleasant to Miss Carteret. I won her trust and she began to confide in me. At last she admitted: 'I do not wish to marry. I do not think the married state would suit me. I would like to leave Mama and set up home in Bath.'

Polite questioning failed to reveal the existence of an admirer, so for a time I was at a loss to understand Miss Carteret's motive. But patience is rewarded and within a few days I was in full possession of the facts surrounding the young lady's life: Lady Dalrymple's bullying, the dreariness of Irish society and the endless bogs and marshes which had made her ill – all these contributed to her desire to remain in Bath when her family returned to Ireland.

She told me of her mother's intransigence and the arrangements being made to find her a husband. 'First one beau and then another:

Mr Elworthy, Captain Brigstock, Mr Elliot and Sir Robert Phelps. I hate them all!'

Innocence and ignorance protected her from recognising the dangers of her own plan. What could she, a pampered pet of a daughter, born to a vain and silly mother, know of the darker side of life? I knew I must dissuade her from acting precipitately, but I did not wish to lose her trust, so I remained silent.

As I moved from client to client, I lent a sympathetic ear to all their aches of body, mind or spirit. I collected news and gossip as I massaged stiff limbs, tended wounds and sores, bathed the bedridden and warmed them on their return from the Baths. I brushed hair, set untidy sick rooms straight, berated lazy servants and made friends of useful ones. Within a fortnight I was in possession of all the latest scandal, who was who in Bath that season, why they were there and with whom they were on visiting terms. I brought each day's catch of news to my sister's kitchen table, where we chewed it over as we sipped tea and enjoyed an hour of leisure together. She would then speak of her tenants. With a dozen rooms at her disposal, Emily had split them up to create six apartments, of varying size and grandeur – not that Westgate Buildings could aspire to the heights of The Crescent, or Laura Place – ours was a more humble clientele.

We could not offer the gardens or shaded walks of the higher town, situated as we were, near the river, but our proximity to the Pump Room more than compensated for these disadvantages and attracted guests of the middling kind. All our larger rooms overlooked the street and tended to be noisy, so Emily had made sitting rooms at the front, with a bedroom lying behind each one. Two of these had windows overlooking the little yard at the back, but the others made do with a high light and no view, which made them a little dark and close in summer. However, they proved more than adequate for the bedridden, if the connecting door was left open during the day.

One tenant, Mrs Richards, usually sat by the open window watching the busy street below, whilst her husband, the retired Major, took the waters for his gout. She always had some needlework near to hand, but seldom picked it up. She would look wistfully at the colourful dresses below her, clearly regretting that she was no longer free to dance and play. I found her a poor source of entertainment, but listening to her complaints and regrets, her sighs and wistful expressions, fed the store of anecdotes I took with me to Mrs Smith, who occupied the cheapest room and whose condition appeared to be taking a turn for the better.

I discovered that Mrs Smith had been in Bath for three weeks before I appeared. She had arrived so ill that my sister had been forced to pay for a nurse to tend her. As she gained strength and began to sit up for an hour in the afternoon, I recognised in her a kindred spirit, moulded by life's vicissitudes. It was clear that she had come down in the world. I suspected that money was short and wondered whether my sister had pressed for the rent.

As movement returned to Mrs Smith's stiff and wasted limbs, my gentle massage and warming cloths, seemed also to unlock her tongue. Bit by bit, I learnt of her marriage (at just nineteen) to a gallant man of property. Money and fast living compensated for lack of genuine love. Sensation, travel and change supplied all their needs until, through the bad influence of one who was wealthier and more reckless than they, the whole tottering pile of cards came crashing down. Mr Smith, hopeless and broken, caught cold and died. Mrs Smith, alone and fearing destitution made one valiant attempt to importune the feckless friend, seeking his assistance and putting herself at his mercy. He cast her off. She succumbed to cold and hunger and, with little left to sustain her, found herself in Bath, friendless, sick and alone – until my sister learnt of her plight and took her in. 'Payment,' she had said, 'could wait.'

That day, wrapped in blankets and resting by the window, Mrs Smith fell silent and turned away from my gaze, ashamed of having said so much. But I would not leave her thus.

'My sister is a kind soul, but she will not be able to keep you here forever. She has her living to make and letting rooms is her only means of doing so. How much do you have left?'

Shocked by my bluntness, Mrs Smith named a pitiful sum.

'It is little enough, but you are growing stronger and I can help you

181

to augment your income.' I thought of Mrs Richard's idle fingers. 'Do you knit or sew?'

She did. 'My hands are far less stiff than last week. I would like to try if I may.'

'I have an hour this afternoon. I will bring patterns and threads and show you how to make pieces to sell.'

And so it began. Mrs Smith was quick to learn. She had not forgotten her youthful lessons with the needle and before long her good days were industrious ones. Gradually, she produced a range of goods which I took with me when I visited my wealthier clients. Her needle cases, card racks and other small items fitted easily into my bag. My patients were glad to buy, passing the pieces off as their own when they gave them as gifts to their friends and acquaintances. So typical of Bath: all show and little substance to their giving, but it did not matter to me. I picked my customers carefully. Miss Carteret bought several pieces, but Mrs Wallis, a very wealthy dowager, became my best customer. Upon her I urged the most expensive fancy-ware and she was generous in her payments.

Mrs Smith was improving. Her income augmented, she was becoming more herself and I began to look upon her as a friend rather than a patient. The hours I spent with her were happy ones and, if she still had the occasional bad day, she was courageous and merry on the days when she felt well and I was confident that, given time and better circumstances, she would recover her health.

Several weeks passed thus. Then, one day, returning full of news, I burst in upon Mrs Smith unannounced and found that she was not alone. Her visitor rose to greet me and was introduced as an old school friend: Anne Elliot.

I curtsied a welcome and went in search of tea, hoping to stem the flow of praise for me from an animated Mrs Smith.

On my return she said: 'Miss Elliot is from Kellynch Hall. She is the cousin of Mr Elliot – of whom I spoke, Nurse Rooke.'

'Mr *William* Elliot?' I said. 'A cousin?'

'Yes,' said Mrs Smith. 'Miss Elliot means to marry him.'

'No!' the lady cried out. 'I said no such thing!'

'But surely, knowing him to be your father's heir, and wealthy, you cannot refuse him if he asks!'

I remembered the near miss on the Bath road and the red faced fury of the driver – his friend had surely called him Elliot? And Miss Carteret – had she not mentioned a Mr Elliot? And Mrs Wallis, who knew of a Mr Elliot who had been seen out walking with a Mrs Clay, said to be the paramour of another man called Elliot – a baronet with three daughters?

Knowledge is power – I believed it!

'Shall I pour you both another cup of tea,' I said, 'I think you may be interested in what I have to say.'

GORGEOUS GEORGE

Deirdre Maher

Kitty's feet hurt. She had been walking for hours and now it was starting to rain again. She was cold and scared, and hungry, and completely lost. The rain turned to hail and the hail pelted down, hopping off the pavement.

'Shit.' Kitty ran towards a telephone box and darted inside. It was too late, she was soaked.

'Shit. Shit. Shit.' She leaned her pale forehead against the streaming glass and began to cry. She thought of the warm bed in the room she shared with her sister and wished with all her heart she was back there. Never again would she complain about sharing. Lydia could make as much mess as she liked, borrow anything she wanted and Kitty would never say a word. She just wanted to go home. Lost and alone, she had never wanted her sister more. After the divorce, and when their mother's drinking got worse, they had grown even closer. Before Jane and Lizzie had moved into the flat together, they had kept things more or less on an even keel, but they didn't live at home anymore, did they? They didn't know the half of it. There had been times when she had wanted to tell them, but Lydia had persuaded her not to.

'They'll fuss so much, Kitty – and start interfering. At least this way we can do what we want.' What Lydia had wanted was to have fun. It had started innocently enough – boys from school, a few beers and the occasional joint. Kitty thought she would do anything to have those days back. When she and Lydia had laughed together at the boys they knew. That was before George had come into their lives.

Before George, the only male attention they had enjoyed had come from boys their own age, spotty and hesitant. But George was different. It wasn't just that he was gorgeous, although he was. Or that he was so much older. When you were with George, he made you feel special and Kitty had never felt special before. She was always the one to be overlooked. Even plain, geeky Mary had a way of getting herself noticed. But Kitty? She had nothing to distinguish her. Neither the youngest nor the tallest; not the prettiest or the wittiest; neither her mother's nor her father's favourite.

'Oh, hang Kitty,' she had heard her mother say. 'What has she to do with anything?'

'You girls mind if we buy you a drink?' The two men had settled themselves in seats beside the girls. Mind? Why would they mind? They were always trying to get served in bars, and not always successfully, even though Lydia looked so much older than her fifteen years. It was Kitty who looked like the youngest sister. Lydia was the taller of the two and Kitty had often wished that her boobs were bigger, like Lydia's. Almost from the first, George had shown more interest in Kitty. He laughed and flirted with Lydia but with Kitty, he was gentle, respectful. For Kitty it was intoxicating. He and his friend, Denny, had been watching them, he said, waiting for an opportunity to introduce themselves. Kitty was impressed. How old fashioned, said Lydia, but she smiled invitingly at both.

That first night in the pub, Lydia told them all about the divorce, their mum, her constant complaints and back biting about Dad, about the empty bottles and the days when she didn't even come out of her room. How they hardly saw Dad because he was busy with his new family.

'You're sure she won't mind you being out so late?' asked George. 'I wouldn't want to get you into trouble.'

Lydia laughed. It came out as a snort, which happened sometimes when she was drunk. 'She's not bothered. We can do what we want. Right, Kitty?'

George looked at Kitty, a warm, friendly, enquiring look. She blushed and stammered a reply.

When Lydia went to the ladies, teetering on her high heels and casting an arch look back over her shoulder at their new companions as she went, George smiled at Kitty.

'Your sister's quite the flirt.' He leaned forward. 'I think you have to work a little harder to get to know the real Kitty. But I bet she's worth knowing.'

He paused for a moment, looking steadily into her eyes. She could feel her heart thudding in her chest.

He had driven them home in an expensive red car.

'Maybe don't tell Mum about this, eh?' he smiled. 'She might not approve of our – friendship.'

Standing in the telephone box, soaked and trembling, Kitty wondered, now, how she could have been fooled. But she had liked him so much and needed so much to believe him. He had kissed her that night, outside the pub, and arranged to meet next day. Lydia was not to know. It might hurt her feelings, he said. No one was to know. He gave her a gift – a little mobile phone, in a pretty pink cover, just so that they could keep in touch with each other. She was walking on air. She could think of nothing but her gorgeous new boyfriend. George liked her better than Lydia. It was hard to believe.

It was difficult to keep it from Lydia, but she thought she had managed it, until last night.

Kitty produced a damp tissue from the pocket of her skirt and blew her nose. Her eye fell on a bright green sticker stuck to the wall of the telephone box.

'CONFUSED? LONELY? NOWHERE TO TURN? Call us for free confidential advice and support...' Someone had scribbled over the 'confidential advice and support' bit and added two extra words. Now it read: 'Call us for a free fuck.'

Even if she did call, what would she say? She had fallen for an older man. She had thought he cared about her, but now she knew he hadn't, that he hadn't cared at all. She had run away from him. She had run away but she didn't know if she had run far enough. She closed her eyes and clenched her fists. Was it only yesterday that it had all gone bad?

It was to be a secret, he'd told her, just between the two of them. He wanted her to meet some 'special friends' of his, old army chums. He asked her to dress up, put on a little make-up.

'Wear that little denim skirt,' he told her, 'I like that one.'

She didn't like being told what to wear, how to look, but she wanted to please him, so she had put it on and was applying her make-up when Lydia had bounced into the room they shared. She flung herself onto her bed and lay there watching, surrounded by the usual mess of crumpled clothes, sweet wrappers and an assortment of eyeliners, shadows and blushers tumbling out of an open cosmetic bag.

'Where are you off to then?' She had asked.

'Just out,' Kitty had replied.

'You're going out with *him*, aren't you?'

'I don't know who you mean.'

'Oh don't try to be clever, Kitty. You know, I didn't think you could be so stupid. You think someone like George could actually be interested in you? Poor, boring Kitty. You know he just wants you for one thing – then he'll dump you.'

Kitty turned to face her. 'You can't bear it that he likes me best. It's killing you. I pity you Lydia. I really do. I wouldn't be you for anything. You're just eaten up with jealousy. If he'd chosen you we would never have heard the end of it. But he didn't, did he? He chose me and you can't bear me to have anything you want.' Kitty turned back to the mirror and with a shaking hand, began to put the final touches to her eyeliner. In a moment she heard the door slam behind her sister.

Maybe it was because of what Lydia had said but from the first that night, Kitty couldn't help noticing that something was different. Surely she was mistaken? It was Lydia's fault for planting doubt in her mind.

'Too much eyeliner,' he had remarked when they met, and handed her a tissue.

They drove through the dark, Kitty chattering nervously. He seemed distant, tense. He interrupted her.

'Listen. When we get there, I'm going to introduce you to a few of my friends, OK? I want you to be nice to them.' Well, of course she would be nice to them, she said – why wouldn't she? He seemed irritated by her answer. 'Don't let me down,' he said. 'I've told them a lot about you.' Kitty was flattered. She told him she would never let him down. He smiled and patted her leg. 'I'm counting on you Kitty.' She had had no idea what he was talking about.

At the party, the room was packed with people. Kitty couldn't help noticing that all the men seemed much older than the girls, and there were more of them. George told her to stay put and she watched him go up to a fat, middle-aged man. They talked for a few minutes and the man looked across at her, then back at George. He nodded and to her surprise, they shook hands. Kitty didn't understand what was happening, but it made her feel uneasy. George came back alone, all smiles.

'How about a drink?' he asked.

'Who is that man?' asked Kitty.

'Just a friend,' he said.

'An army friend?'

'A what? Oh – yeah. An old army buddy. Listen, Kitty. The thing is, I owe him some money and well, I wondered if you might help. You know, just spend a bit of time with him, be nice to him for a while – then we can get out of here and spend some time together.'

Kitty couldn't believe her ears. Be nice to that fat old man. What did that mean? She felt sick and dizzy.

'Where's the bathroom?' she asked. She couldn't think straight. He brought her upstairs and led her to a door. On the way they passed other men. Most of them nodded at George and gave her hard, appraising stares. At last she slipped into the bathroom and closed the door behind her. There was no lock. She looked at her face in the mirror. She saw the face of a little girl playing at being grown up, smudged eyeliner and too much lipstick. Lydia was right. Why would someone like George want her? Did he even want her for himself? The thought brought another wave of sickness. It couldn't be true, she refused to believe it. She took a deep breath and moved reluctantly to the door. Slowly, she began to open it. She stopped when she heard Denny's voice.

'Why didn't you bring the pretty one?' Denny was asking.

'Too much like hard work,' she heard George reply. 'Besides, not desperate enough.'

Kitty stood motionless. It was as if everything inside her had shut down, leaving only the sound of their voices echoing in her head. *Why didn't you bring the pretty one? Not desperate enough. Desperate enough…*

191

The door opened inwards with a push and she stepped back. 'Finished?' She nodded, pretending to adjust her skirt. She could feel their eyes watching her. She lifted her gaze and managed a smile.

'If I'm nice to him, can we go then?' She asked as they went downstairs.

'Sure, sure,' he replied. 'Let's get a drink first.' But she saw how his eyes slid away from hers, already searching the crowd for his 'friend.' Kitty didn't know how she did it, but she made it to the bottom of the stairs and kept smiling. All the time her stomach lurched and his hand in the small of her back burned through her skimpy top. She felt small and defenceless, acutely aware of unwelcome male scrutiny. The first shock of betrayal was wearing off, replaced by a sickening fear.

'Wait here.' He disappeared into the first room again and left her in the hallway. The front door was open. Two men stood blocking the entrance. They were drunk and seemed to be arguing. One of the men began to shout at the other, shoving him hard in the chest so that the second man stumbled back. Kitty could see the path, and beyond, an open gate. She didn't think, she just ran, out the door and down the path, out the gate and down the road. She ran and ran until her breath gave out and then she hid in someone's garden until she was sure there was no one in pursuit. She had no idea where she was or how long she'd crouched there, numb with misery. Eventually she emerged and began to walk.

Now she looked out of the telephone box at the dawn light in the sky and noticed that the hail had stopped. Her feet squelched in her sodden pumps. She took a deep breath, picked up the phone and dialled the number on the bright green sticker.

Kitty was dry and cosy and warm, wrapped up in her duvet on the sofa, snuggled up between Jane and Lizzie. She had been expecting a scene of mammoth proportions when the police brought her home, but it hadn't been like that at all. Jane had cried and hugged her tight. Lizzie had held both her hands tightly, her eyes suspiciously bright and had shaken her head at her; 'Oh, Kitty, I am so sorry,' she had said. Kitty had been puzzled by this but allowed herself to be led gently away to a hot bath. Only Mary and her mother were absent from the family circle.

Her father had been gruff but not angry and had listened in silence as she told the police officers what she knew. There was a young woman officer and a tall man with a big nose who seemed to be in charge. They had nodded and exchanged glances when she began to describe George and afterwards the officer with the big nose had looked serious and taken her father aside for a few words. Kitty had strained to hear – but all she could catch was the odd phrase: 'known to us' and 'previous record'. She had heard about 'grooming' but had never really thought about it before. Why should she? Now it seemed that George had been 'grooming' her. It was something he had done before. She hadn't been the first. She didn't even have that to distinguish her. 'You're one of the lucky ones,' they told her.

But Kitty didn't feel lucky. Lydia's welcoming words still burned in her ears. 'Poor Kitty,' she had whispered in mock sympathy, her eyes bright with triumph. 'See, he hadn't wanted you at all.'

BIOGRAPHIES

(In alphabetical order)

Sarah Baillie is twenty-six years old, and from the United Kingdom. She gained a degree in English Language & Literature from the University of Leeds before surprising her friends and family by becoming a midwife. Sarah has been reading and writing stories since childhood and, thanks to her mother's good taste, grew up with a love for all things Austen. Being an eldest sister herself, Sarah holds a special place in her heart for Elinor Dashwood, but her current favourite of Jane Austen's works is *Persuasion*.

'A Thing of Beauty' is Sarah's first published piece of writing.

Eithne Cullen was born in Dublin, and her family moved to London when she was six years old. An avid reader, Eithne takes great pleasure from her reading group which encourages an eclectic mix of books. She likes to write stories and poems. She lives with her husband in East London, and works close to home. She is unashamedly proud of her three grown up children, and endeavours to embarrass them as often as she can.

As a mature student **Mary Fitzpatrick** studied English at the University of Glasgow; after graduating she taught English to both children and adults. She has completed an Open University creative writing course, which really helped her to focus; she has also attended numerous short writing courses, including one run by the Arvon Foundation. Mary has recently moved back to Glasgow from rural Dumfries and Galloway and is loving the buzz of city life; going to the cinema, theatre and just basically soaking up the atmosphere of the streets. She is also taking more creative writing classes, the most recent through Strathclyde University.

Marian Ford studied French at Manchester University and has worked in London and Grenoble. She has edited graduate careers literature and written restaurant reviews. In 2012, Marian won the *Hampshire Chronicle* short story competition and celebrated by embarking on an MA in Creative and Critical Writing at Winchester University. As a writer based in Winchester she is sometimes tempted to stalk Jane Austen's ghost. She has been known to loiter outside Jane's former house in College Street, listening for the sound of shrewd laughter and the echo of footsteps on distant cobbles.

Clare Girvan lives in a pretty Devon estuary town with her three cats. She has won prizes in many short story competitions, including the Ian St James, Fish and Asham Awards, but now concentrates chiefly on writing plays, which vary in length from one to ninety minutes and have had readings and performances in various locations around the country. Her ambition is to have a full length play performed to huge acclaim in a London theatre. She decorates Fabergé-style eggs, works a very small garden and runs a local Craft Fair at Christmas. See website: www.claregirvan.co.uk

As a seminary student, **Price Grisham** followed some valuable advice: 'Ten minutes before turning out the light, read something YOU want to read'; which was Austen.

When he discovered that Austen's great-uncle, Oxford University's Vice Chancellor, tossed the wildly popular clergyman George Whitefield from campus, Grisham's Master's thesis on Austen and the 18th Century Anglican Church not only bumped up his grade point average considerably – but resulted in two television commentaries and three award-winning essays sponsored by the Jane Austen Society of North America. He is a member of the historic Salem Atheneum in Massachusetts, and in May of 2015 was asked by the Chawton House Library to present his paper, 'Serious Subjects: Jane Austen's Barometric Readings of the Anglican Church' at their symposium, 'Religion and Literature in the Long Eighteenth Century'. He is also, humbly, the only male contributor to be included in this anthology;

and when he is not mentoring local college students, is expanding his thesis into a book.

Marybeth Ihle studied English literature at Binghamton University, with her honours thesis focusing on Jane Austen and film adaptations. She earned a master's degree in communications from Georgetown University and studied playwriting in London. She is a member of the New York Metropolitan Region of the Jane Austen Society of North America and its Juvenilia group. She has adapted Jane Austen's unfinished manuscript *The Watsons* into a screenplay, and her short story 'In the Way of Happiness' was published as part of the 2011 Jane Austen Short Story Award. She has spent several memorable holidays in England, where she's wandered the gardens of Hartfield, dined at Uppercross, and danced at Longbourn.

Pamela Holmes wrote her first book at the age of ten; it was about the Mice family. She rises early to write fiction and has recently completed her first novel, which is represented by the literary agent Laura Morris. Pamela is now working on a collection of short stories. The Jane Austen Short Story Award is her first prize. A professional campaigner for the rights of older people, she is the mother of two sons and lives in London with her husband.

Janet Lee lives with her family in Gympie, Australia. She has degrees in journalism and government and is currently a doctoral candidate at the University of the Sunshine Coast. In her thesis she is examining the relationship between Jane Austen and her sister Cassandra.

Although this is her first attempt at fan fiction, Janet has been a Janeite since Mr Darcy stepped out of the lake at Pemberley.

Beginning in 2009, **Elisabeth Lenckos** spent three months as a Fellow at Chawton House Library, a stay that changed her life. An award-winning instructor at the University of Chicago and academic author, she decided to try her hand at fiction after she met Lindsay Ashford. Dr Lenckos holds a doctorate in Comparative Literature and divides her time between London, Chicago, and Berlin. She is currently writing a book on Marian Hastings, the wife of the first Governor General of Bengal.

Deirdre Maher is a dedicated Austen fan, so to be chosen as one of the finalists in this year's Jane Austen Short Story Award competition was a real thrill. She has enjoyed some modest success with her short stories, and was the winner of the ABCtales online prose competition in February 2012 under the pen name Judy Gee. Deirdre is married and lives in London, and is happiest when immersed in a writing project. In future she hopes to devote more time to writing and less time to procrastination.

Leslie McMurtry was born in Albuquerque and lives in London. Her poetry has been published by Gomer, *Poetry Wales*, and *Borderlines*. In 2009 she was awarded a grant, by the Elizabeth George Foundation, to write a screenplay about the life of John Milton. She was longlisted for the Jane Austen Short Story Competition in 2011 and is currently writing a collection of short stories thematically linked to Jane Austen. She holds an MA in creative writing and a PhD in English (radio drama) from Swansea University.

Sandy Norris is a retired English teacher who began to take literature seriously at the age of thirteen, when she read *Pride and Prejudice* for the first time. She now spends much of her week writing and has just completed her first novel. In combining two interests – sailing and naval historical fiction, Sandy has already written a children's historical adventure story: *Run Away to Danger* – set on Henry VIII's ship the *Mary Rose* and this was published by the National Maritime Museum in 2005. She is currently engaged in writing a self-help book for parents struggling to cope with their teenagers.

Susan Piper was born and raised in Canada. In New York and London, she studied acting. She now teaches Music and French at a local primary school. The children inspire stories and make her heart sing.

Susan has lived in Hampshire for twenty-four years with her patient, encouraging partner, a tree surgeon. They recently moved into a little cabin in the woods, having given tenancy of the family house to the two grown up children she is so proud of. Next to the cabin is an even littler 'room of her own' so she has no excuse for not finishing that book!

Sarah Shaw's stories have been published in *Mslexia*, the *London Magazine* and the *Yellow Room*, among other magazines and anthologies. Her short fiction has won first prize in the Ilkley Literature Festival competition, been shortlisted for an Asham Award and won the 2009 New Writing North Badenoch Fiction Award. Shaw's novel, *Make it Back* (2009), was published by Tonto Books. She lives in the North East and has recently gained a PhD in Creative Writing at Northumbria University: her practice-based research involved completing another novel, together with a critical commentary on the process.

Fiona Skepper works as a criminal law solicitor in Melbourne, Australia. She has studied writing, and published short stories in magazines and anthologies and online, and travel articles in magazines and newspapers. She is currently working on a novella. She fell in love with Jane Austen when she was nine and was introduced to *Pride and Prejudice*. She tries to write about many things but specialises in crime fiction. She thinks crimes in fiction tend to be more interesting than the ones she deals with at work.

A retired teacher, **Anne Thomas** lives with her husband Peter in a Somerset rectory, where she supports his work in five rural villages. She loves books and runs two book clubs, and a charity bookstall. She makes time for reading, writing, painting, promoting Fairtrade and sharing her love of Jane Austen.

With twin sons, now in their twenties, she became fascinated by multiple birth children and has worked as an Education Consultant to Tamba (the Twins and Multiple Births Association) for nearly two decades.

She is currently working on a 'true-life novel' set in nineteenth-century London and St Petersburg.

Emily Ruth Verona received her Bachelor of Arts in Creative Writing and Cinema Studies from The State University of New York at Purchase. She is the recipient of the 2014 Pinch Literary Award in Fiction. Her work has been featured in *Read. Learn. Write.*, *Fifty Word Stories*, the *Toast*, and *Popmatters*. She lives in New Jersey.

The Asian Women's Writers Collective was **Jocelyn Watson**'s first writing home. She is one of the Alumni of the Cultural Leadership Programme and was funded to attend the Jaipur Literature Festival in 2011. In 2013 she was the winner of the UK Asian Writer Short Story Competition for 'the Gardener' and in 2011 the winner of the Freedom From Torture Short Story Competition for 'London Plane'. In 2012 she was one of the winners of the SAMPAD 'Inspired by Tagore' competition for 'Loud Music' and the Asian Writer Short Story Prize for 'Sweet and Sour Masala'. She is active in feminist, BME and socialist politics.

LE Yates grew up in Manchester during the 1980s but has lived in Norwich since she came to study the Creative Writing MA at UEA in 2005. Her short stories have appeared in anthologies from *Parenthesis* to *Tessellate* and she has been an Associate Lecturer in Creative Writing at the Open University since 2007.

She won a place on the 2013 Escalator scheme and was awarded an Arts Council grant to complete her novel, *From the Mountains Descended Night*. This explores one of the biggest literary scandals of the eighteenth century – the notorious forger James Macpherson and *The Poems of Ossian*.

Her twitter account is @l_e_yates

Her website is http://leyates.co.uk

THE EDITORS

Lindsay Ashford is the author of seven crime and historical novels. She has also edited several short story collections. *The Mysterious Death of Miss Austen* was dramatised for BBC Radion 4 in 2014 and has since been optioned for television. Her latest book, *The Color of Secrets*, was published in the USA and UK in April 2015 with German and Turkish Translations due out later this year.

Caroline Oakley has worked on the previous two volumes of Chawton House Award winning stories as editor at Honno Press. She has worked in publishing for almost three decades and still reads for fun.

ABOUT HONNO

Honno Welsh Women's Press was set up in 1986 by a group of women who felt strongly that women in Wales needed wider opportunities to see their writing in print and to become involved in the publishing process. Our aim is to develop the writing talents of women in Wales, give them new and exciting opportunities to see their work published and often to give them their first 'break' as a writer. Honno is registered as a community co-operative. Any profit that Honno makes is invested in the publishing programme. Women from Wales and around the world have expressed their support for Honno. Each supporter has a vote at the Annual General Meeting. For more information and to buy our publications, please write to Honno at the address below, or visit our website: www.honno.co.uk

Honno, 14 Creative Units, Aberystwyth Arts Centre
Aberystwyth, Ceredigion SY23 3GL

Honno Friends
We are very grateful for the support of the Honno Friends: Jane Aaron, Annette Ecuyere, Audrey Jones, Gwyneth Tyson Roberts, Beryl Roberts, Jenny Sabine.

For more information on how you can become a Honno Friend, see:
http://www.honno.co.uk/friends.php